THE END
AND
THE BEGINNING

BY

MRS. ANNE MAUREEN YEATES

Published by New Generation Publishing in 2021

First Edition

ISBN 978-1-80031-261-6

www.newgeneration-publishing.com

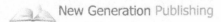 New Generation Publishing

This story is dedicated to my three sons who have autism and severe learning problems.
They are my world

CHAPTER ONE

THE SEA SPRITES

A long time ago in a place called Middle Earth, a time when Elves, Fairies, Witches and Goblins walked this planet, there lived a race of people called Sea Sprites, they looked in appearance like Mortals, but could not breathe air, they could only survive under water and if out of water too long, then they would die...

The Queen of this under water race was pregnant and due to have her baby any time now, but, what the Queen didn't know, was that the infant she was carrying, was to grow up to be a very important person to this world beneath the sea!

The Queen whose name was Corali, was talking to her husband King Danus and they were discussing their child, trying to think up names for when it was born.

How about Demitrious for a boy, said Danus, " no," said Corali, it's going to be a girl and we shall name her Leandra, they talked about it for hours, but, could not agree at all. The King said, my boy is going to grow up big and strong, perfect in every way and so handsome, he is going to be a great warrior and leader of men and he will never shame us or let us down in any way, he will be a man to be proud of and we always will be! The Queen said, " No," it will be a Girl and she will be beautiful and gentle, but, at the same time, strong and proud and she will take her rightful place as Queen of the seas, she will be a fair and just ruler to her people and they will love her ....

Since neither could make up their minds on what the child was to be, or what it was to be named, they decided to consult the Sea Witch to see if she could settle their argument, for she saw all and knew all, if any one could tell them just what the future held in store for them and their child it would be the Witch and no one else!! It was getting dark by the time that they reached the Witches cave where the Witch had made her home for many years now, there were shadows making eerie pictures on the walls and great clumps of smelly seaweed hung around them, it was all a bit scary and they had difficulty in paying attention to what the Witch was saying to them, they couldn't take their eyes off the shadows dancing on the walls and all the eerie shapes, not to mention all the oddly shaped bottles standing on shelves all around the cave ...

At last, they both settled down slightly and began to listen in earnest to what she told them, in about six weeks time, the Witch said, you will have a baby girl, but, she will be no ordinary girl, in that I do not mean that she will be in any way deformed, " no indeed, she will be perfect in every way, her eyes will be Blue and her hair Golden Yellow she will have much great beauty, but, she will not be for our race, she is meant for a greater purpose, a purpose which our race will never see, for when this child reaches the age to bear a child herself then our race will be no more, we will have reached the end of our allotted time in Middle Earth and will no longer exist!!

For your child, who is to be named Nattisa, is to be the Mother of an entirely new race, but, only at the cost of our race, which at this moment in time is all the information that I can give to you about her!!

When the Witch had told the Royal couple all that she knew about the child that they were expecting, she rose up and without further comment she walked out, leaving behind a very confused couple of people, " what on earth did she mean by that," said Corali? " I don't know replied Danus, I didn't understand a word that she said, all I understood was that we are going to have a Girl and that she is to be called Nattisa, all the rest was lost on me it was like the wind rushing through my ears, said Damus, I could not grasp nor hold on to the meaning of what was said to us... ".

I felt the same way, said Corali, I too neither knew or understood what the Evil Witch said, does she mean that our child is to be an assassin who will destroy all her race including us that got together through love and created her!

"I think that the stupid woman must be ill if that's what she meant, for no child that we have conceived would ever grow up to be a murderer, if I thought that then I would banish her from the kingdom or hide her away from the world in which she would be a threat and a danger, " I would even destroy: her myself if I thought that she could be a killer... "No," said Danus, " I will not have it that our sweet unborn child could ever do an evil deed, the Witch must have meant something else, although what I do not know for her words were like a foreign language to me, we shall just have to wait and see, perhaps in time it will all be made clear to us just what she was trying to tell us!

They left the cave hand in hand with a puzzled expression on their faces, two very mixed up people indeed and how they wished that above all else they had not come to the Witch this night to ask about their baby, though both of them knew deep down that their child could not be a killer and that the Witch must have meant something else, when she said that their child was to be the Mother of a new race, but, only at the cost of their race, how they wished that they knew what she meant, but, only time would answer that...

In the next few weeks however, things were rather hectic and they forgot what the Witch had told them, they were too busy preparing for the new arrival, well let's just say they didn't really forget, but, pushed it to the back of their minds because they didn't want to think about it, they really wanted to forget that the whole thing happened ... The next six weeks just flew over and before Corali and Danus knew it, the child that they had long waited for was finally here being born into this underwater world! It was a hard birth being the Queen's first and though she didn't know it at the time her last baby, but, when she looked down at the Blue eyed, Blonde haired infant who was nestling in the crook of her arms it was worth all the pain just to finally see the child who had been growing and nourishing for so long now inside of her ....

3

"Hello Nattisa my beloved one, "oh no, you are never going to be a killer of men, a breaker of hearts maybe, but, not a killer, you are the creation of two great hearts beating as one, of a love more vast than the Heavens and you will never harm anyone. As I look into your precious eyes and see the love and trust there within them, I know that you will be a great person when you grow to be an adult and I weep that I will not be there to see you, but, for now my sweet one you are mine ...

The Queen was left alone with her new baby for a while, it was called the bonding time where both Mother and child got to know each other and grow together as they should do, then the Midwife ushered King Danus into the room warning him not to stay too long as both Mother and baby needed plenty of rest, they had both had a long hard struggle and were in need of a good long sleep ....

The King came slowly up to the bed, he peeped down at his new born infant lying so quiet and serene in his wife's arms, is this my child that you hold so lovingly and gentle, asked Danus, or is it some Angel that you have stolen from paradise just for me! Little did he know that Nattisa would not look so serene and angelic for long, for as she grew up, she would be a Holy terror with mischief as her middle name ....

The Queen was ordered complete bed rest for a few days as the birth had been a rather bad one, Nattisa had been a big baby with a bonny birth weight, but, after a few days of rest and the good care of the Midwife, she was allowed home with her baby.

The Royal couple left the birth confinement cave as a real Family at last and in those first few days they just delighted in the gift of this precious child, life was one long round of feeding and changing and playing with Nattisa, they were getting to know their baby daughter and nothing else mattered, the city was left to rule it's self....

Nattisa had a beautiful nursery to sleep in and it was filled with playthings for when she got older, there were colourful shells of all shapes and sizes and corals of every hue and colour, red and green seaweed hung from the walls and a carpet of soft fresh green seaweed fronds as a carpet for her to play on when she could walk...

Her crib was a giant Clam and the King had made her a potty from a large Snail shell, being a Princess she had everything that she wanted, but, it didn't spoil her at all, for once she was past the childish phase Nattisa grew up to be polite and caring of others When Nattisa was two months old she was presented before the people of Coral City which her parents ruled fairly and wisely, there was a huge celebration and a great feast was held in her honour, all the Sprites in the kingdom attended, but, there was food and drink enough for them all and everyone had a grand time.

The people all lined up to see Nattisa and to pay her homage, they had wanted to see her since the day that she was born, but, that had been impossible, so they had, had to be patient until Nattisa was old enough and strong enough to be presented to them....

The Sprites were delighted with their new Princess, they said that she was just about the most beautiful baby that they had ever seen and all of them drank to toast her health " Isn't she good, said one Sprite to her friend, " yes a real Angel, replied her friend, little did they know that they would have cause to take back their words, for as she grew up anyone would have thought twice before calling her an Angel again, for Nattisa became mischief incarnate and got up to all kinds of trouble !!

The months after the Royal feast, just seemed to fly over and Nattisa grew fast, she was a very quick child and intelligent, she soon learned how to swim, walk and talk, and before her first birthday, could put words together to make a sentence. Her first birthday party was also a great feast day, all the people bought her gifts, and again they all had a wonderful day, the party had been going on for a few hours, when Queen Corali, noticed that Nattisa was missing, she had wandered off unnoticed by any of the guests, there was then a great commotion, and everyone was dashing about here, there and everywhere, looking for the Princess!

5

The King and Queen were beside themselves with worry, but they needn't have concerned themselves, for Nattisa was found in the Royal Palace gardens nearby, she was sitting in the Oyster beds, and had gorged herself on the Oysters, till she was sick! When she was found by the Palace Guards, her face was a horrid green colour, and her eyes were bulging and bloodshot, she was heaving, and trying to be sick, her poor parents didn't know whether to laugh or cry, when they found out where she'd been, and what she'd been up to, needless to say Nattisa never touched another Oyster for ages after that, but she didn't stop getting into trouble, she was always up to some trick or another, that day on her first birthday, had been just the start of a long string of things, that Nattisa would do, to worry and annoy her parents!

Nattisa was swimming with her little friend Marnie, one day, she was nearly two years old now and her friend was a little older, they both stopped swimming when they noticed something on the sea floor, they went to have a closer look as it was an animal that they had never seen before, the animal was dark grey in colour and was oval in shape, it had long trailing tentacles, and was all covered in lumps, the tentacles were covered in strong suckers, the animal was all squashy and squidgy when they touched it, and neither child knew what it could be.

Between them both, they lifted the animal gently to examine it more closely, but the animal must have been frightened by them, because it squirted a spray of some jet black stuff at them, which they later learned was ink.

The animal, which they learned was an Octopus, shot away from them in fear, leaving them both covered from head to toe, in this foul smelling stuff!

When they both arrived home, the only thing visible', was their eyes, when Queen Corali saw Nattisa coming home in this state, she was so angry, she ranted and raved, but when she saw how down Nattisa was, she saw the funny side of the situation, and started to laugh, when Nattisa had been cleaned up, her Mother sat her down and explained to her about the creature, that she had encountered, Corali told her child, that there were many creatures in the sea, some were funny like the Octopus, some were beautiful like the different fishes, but some were dangerous, and were to be feared and kept well away from, like the most dangerous of all, the SHARK!

CHAPTER TWO

NATTISA GROWING UP

The incident with the Octopus was soon forgotten, for other things quickly pushed it into the background, for as Nattisa grew she was learning all the time, she learned all about the creatures, that her Mother told her about, and she found out that she had a great understanding with these creatures!

She rode on the backs of the Dolphins, and the Manta Rays young offspring, and it was through this that she got into her next lot of trouble, she had been playing with a Dolphin, when she spotted a young Manta Ray, it had got itself trapped between two rocks, and was crying out in pain!

Nattisa and the Dolphin went over to see if they could get the poor thing free, they had just managed to free it, when from behind them came an awful noise, they turned just in time to see the Mother of the young Manta Ray rushing towards them, she was huge and looked very angry, she had heard her little one crying, and thought that Nattisa and her Dolphin friend were trying to hurt her baby!

They just had time to dive into a nearby cave, when the creature hurtled down apon them with such fury, that the rush of water that she created, knocked them right to the back of the cave, and completely winded them!

The Manta Ray dived up and down in front of the cave, such hate and fury in the noises that she was making, that they knew if she could have got to them, then she would have killed them, and that was when Nattisa swore that she would never try to help another trapped creature as long as she lived, but she didn't really mean it, it was just the fear inside her, that made Nattisa swear this oath, for in the years that followed Nattisa was to help many more trapped and wounded creatures. The Manta Ray swam up and down in front of the cave nearly all day, waiting for them to come out, how they wished that she would go away, they had, had nothing to eat all day and were famished, but no way would they come out of the cave, not with the angry mother dashing up and down past the cave mouth, Nattisa said to her Dolphin friend, well, friend Blip, if we can't get out of the front of the cave I wonder if there is a back way out, they began to search the back of the cave for a way out, but it was just a dead end, so they knew that, they would just have to wait till the angry Mother, gave up and went away!

They had just resigned themselves to waiting out the night, when they heard shouts in the distance, it was the palace guards searching for them, the King and Queen had been so worried about their daughter not coming home, that they had started a search party for the missing Princess, once again, she was just Five years old, when this incident happened, the guards were making that much noise, shouting for the Princess, that the Manta Ray took flight, she would have stopped and fought them, but they were too many for her to beat, so she gave an angry look to the Princess and left!

When Nattisa knew that the angry creature had finally gone she came out of the cave followed closely by her friend Blip, she was never as glad to see the palace guards and her Mother and Father in the whole of her short life...

The King and Queen rushed up to their daughter and hugged her," where on earth have you been Nattisa," her Mother said, we have been looking everywhere for you, we were so worried when you didn't come home for your meal and both her parents cried at the sheer relief at having found their daughter alive and well!

Nattisa told them the whole story of how she helped the trapped baby Manta Ray and of how the Mother thought that she and Blip were hurting her baby, then she told of being trapped in the cave all these long hours and of having nothing to eat since breakfast this morning, her Mother really cried then, "oh Nattisa, she said, don't you know that you could have been killed, why do you do these things and why do you hurt us so!! "

"I don't know Mother, replied Nattisa, I don't mean to do these things, " I don't mean to worry you or hurt you, I just can't help it, these things seem to happen to me without me really wanting them to, " I am ever so sorry Mummy, but, I can't promise not to do these things again for I don't think that is in my power to do so....

The King turned to his wife, "come along Corali, he said, let us get our child home and feed and bathe her, for if the words of the Witch are true then we know that no harm can truly befall her, has not the Witch told us that Nattisa will be the only one left of our race, now let us take her home and see to her needs for we can not wrap her up in soft seaweed to protect her, we know that what is to be will be and there is nothing that we can do to stop it no matter how much we may want to do.

When they arrived back at Coral City with the Princess all safe and sound they were greeted with cheers of relief for the entire city had come out to watch for them, in the crowd were the two women who had thought how angelic Nattisa had looked as a baby, now they sang a different tune, "what a Devil our Princess is, said one of the women to her friend, that she should put her parents and all her people through such worry," why doesn't the selfish Princess realise that one day she will be crowned Queen and rule the whole of Coral City, if she survives that long that is, what then will become of us should anything happen to her, " why does she our future ruler put herself into danger like this, " why doesn't she behave herself and act like a princess should for I fear that we shall be left with no one to rule us, if she doesn't mend her wandering ways and learn to act with dignity and behave like a member of the Royalty is supposed to, "yes and I thoroughly agree with all that you say, replied the woman's friend.....

As they were speaking the Royals passed them by and both women bowed their heads in respect of them, for even though they spoke of Nattisa that way it was not out of scorn for their Princess, but, out of fear for themselves in case they were robbed of their future ruler, for they would be like a boat without a paddle, adrift in high seas if they were left with no one to rule them and whether they liked it or not Nattisa was to be their future ruler, that is if they survived that long!!

The next few months after the Manta Ray event were fairly quiet, but, not too quiet, Nattisa was trying her best to be on her best behaviour, there were a few small incidents like the time that she decided to decorate her bedroom, but not telling her parents about her idea, she collected together all the different colours that she could...

From shells she got red and orange, from seaweed she got green, blue and mauve, from sea urchins and anemones she got yellow and gold, when she had finally collected all the colours that she needed, Nattisa got on with the work of painting with them! Her Mother got the shock of her life when she came to tell Nattisa that it was time for her evening meal, the whole room was like a vast rainbow with a mixture of all the colours and Nattisa was sat there in the middle of it all, she was covered from head to toe in all the different shades of colours, unless you looked for her closely, you would swear that she was a part of the wall, her Mother only noticed her when she moved ....

"Nattisa," her mother said angrily, " what have you been up to now," Nattisa smiled up happily at her Mother and all the Queen could see was a row of pearly white teeth in a mass of many colours, " I thought my room was looking rather dull, said Nattisa, so I thought that I would brighten it up a bit, " brighten it up yes," her Mother said, but, did you have to use every colour under the sea, why it looks revolting, she said, " oh I think that it looks lovely smiled Nattisa, "well it doesn't," replied the Queen, now come along while I clean you up, then you can have your meal and while we are doing that, we shall see what the palace decorator can do about restoring your room....

"Oh Mother, said Nattisa, " don't you," oh Mother me, said the Queen, but, I like it this way, Nattisa moaned, I think it's just beautiful, "well I don't, said her Mother angrily, so you'll just have to get used to it in one colour and she dragged Nattisa off to be cleaned up, while sending off a message to the palace decorator to fix the room. When Nattisa had been cleaned and had eaten her meal, she went out to play with her friend Marnie and her Dolphin friend Blip, they had a great time riding on Blip's back and she told Marnie all about her Mother being such a spoilsport, for not letting her keep her bedroom in all those lovely colours, " you should have seen it Marnie, Nattisa said, "it was wonderful, I would have loved to have slept in my room of many colours, " I don't know replied Marnie, perhaps your Mother was right, I mean Mothers are supposed to be always right at least that's what they tell us, "they are always saying Mother knows best you know or else they say I'm your Mother I know what is best for you and it may have given you nightmares anyway sleeping in a room of so many colours, " maybe you're right Marnie, Nattisa said, maybe it is for the best , well I think that I'll go in and see how my room is coming on, I'll see you two later, she said, to her friends..

She opened the curtain to her bedroom and peeped in, what a lovely surprise she got, her room had been done in the most gorgeous Coral Pink and all around the walls hung coloured anemones," oh how lovely, cried Nattisa, she was glad that her mother had known what was best for her, or she wouldn't have this lovely room to sleep in tonight, she would have been sleeping in a room of many nightmarish colours!

The months flew over with Nattisa getting up to just the usual childish things, when before her parents realised it her Seventh birthday was here, don't the days and years just fly over, said Corali, to her husband Danus, it doesn't seem two minutes since she was born and now here, she is on her Seventh birthday, " I know, said Danus, you wonder just where the time and the years are vanishing to ...

We shall be holding a party again I presume, said Corali, "yes!' said Danus, but, only for Nattisa's young friends, we cannot hold a party for all the kingdom for every year that is her birthday, besides, the people of the city wouldn't expect to come to her birthday every year surely, "I don't know replied Corali, but, I wouldn't want to offend our people in any way or make them feel left out of anything!

"No I'm sure we wouldn't offend them, Danus said, they must know that we can only invite them to special birthday parties for Nattisa, not every year, I think the people will understand if the Princess only wants to invite a few of her close friends to her party, "no," he said, " I'm positive that the people would not be offended!!

"But, he was wrong, the people of the city were deeply offended and they didn't blame their King and Queen for not being invited to the Royal party, they blamed Nattisa, the whole of the city said, what a spoilt selfish Princess she was, not to want her people with her on her birthday, but, they were only thinking of themselves, for the Sea Sprites were a childish race of people who thought only of themselves, they knew that they would be missing out on a feast of great food and drink, at that moment in time that was all they cared about, so for months after the party the people of the city sulked with their Princess, like silly children they refused to bow their heads in respect as she passed them by, and after she had passed them they muttered to each other angrily about her, although Nattisa never knew this for they never let her see them do this angry muttering and she never noticed when they bent their heads down to her anyway, so the Princess never knew that she had angered her people by not inviting them to her party, but, her parents knew that they were angry with Nattisa and they were ashamed of their people...

"Why do the people treat our daughter with such disrespect, the Queen asked her husband? " Because they were not invited to her party, answered the King, and because they are silly and childish people who have not grown up yet and may never will, perhaps they shall come to regret their treatment of her in the future, said Danus, but, perhaps they will not live that long to regret anything, for if what the Witch has told us is to come true, I think that we should take each day as it comes and make the most of our lives while we still have a life to live, before it is too late!!

So saying this, Danus took hold of his Wife's hand and holding his head up high, he proudly walked past the stupid people that he and Corali ruled together and caught up with Nattisa!

As time went by, the people, forgot all about the party, in fact being rather slow witted people, they couldn't even remember, why they had been angry with their Princess, so they stopped being angry with her, and just got on with their lives.

But, the King and Queen, never made the mistake of leaving out the people again, and every time it was Nattisa's birthday, the Royal couple declared a day of enjoyment, and laid on a great feast for their people, so they were never angry with Nattisa, again!

Nattisa was growing up fast now, and was altering with every year that past, she was turning into a polite and well-mannered young woman, and her parents were really proud of the way, that she was turning out, in fact they had always been proud of her!

The young Princess, was turning into a real beauty, and had many a lad turning their head, looking hopefully in her direction, but it was not to be, she was not interested in them. She spent her days, riding her Dolphin friend Blip, and exploring the sea, and her nights were spent learning things, because, she didn't want to turn out to be as slow witted, as the people, that she would one day rule over, she wanted to rise above them, so that, she could rule them wisely, as her parents were doing now!

It was on one of these exploration trips, that Nattisa, had her first deadly encounter, with the much feared Shark, and the encounter, turned out rather sadly for her friend Blip. They were swimming in a deep part of the sea, where Nattisa hadn't been before, when out of the gloomy depths, came a large grey shape gliding towards them.

It was huge, and it was an animal that Nattisa had never seen before, but she knew from her Mother's description of it, that the huge creature could only be a Shark!

She and Blip, stayed perfectly still, they didn't move a muscle, as much through fear as anything else, the Shark circled slowly around them, gliding through the water without making so much as one ripple, considering the size of the creature!

It's eyes were fixed and staring, but they knew that it saw them, as it swam the Shark came closer, and they sensed, rather than knew, that it was smelling their fear, and that smell of fear, was exiting the creature into attacking them.

Suddenly, it closed in on them, and without warning it attacked, as it gnashed out with it's huge jaws, Blip darted sidewards, and as Nattisa wasn't expecting this move, she fell off her friends back, and felt herself falling to the sea floor.

So she drifted downwards, for she was too afraid to swim, as any sudden move, might have caused the Shark, to attack again, but, Nattisa saw, that she didn't need to move, to make the creature attack again, it was coming at her anyway, it's huge jaws closing in on her, were the last thing she saw, as her head hit a rock, and she blacked out!

As Nattisa lay prone, on the sea floor, the Shark came in for the kill, and as it did, Blip gathered up his courage and charged at the creature, to save his friend from certain death, a dreadful battle then took place, between the two creatures.

Blip charged the Shark, over and over, hitting it in the gills, with his hard nose, but the huge Shark didn't go down without a fight, it bit the Dolphin terribly and thrashed out at him, with it's tail, till finally it lay still, the Shark lay dying, it's life blood gushing out through it's gills, onto the bed of the sea floor!

The Shark was dead, but, Blip had not escaped unscathed, he was mortally wounded, and as he lay dying , he looked at his lifelong, childhood friend, who he had given up his life for, and he did not regret a moment, of what he had done to save Nattisa, from certain death, he made a sad gurgling sound, as he choked on his own blood, once again he looked over at his friend, she was the last thing, that he ever saw in this world, as he slowly slipped away, into the next world, and lay still, gently rocking, with the sea current! It was all over by the time Nattisa came around, she looked rather stunned, and bewildered, at first, she didn't know where she was, or what, had happened, she was lost and confused, then everything came back to her, she looked around rather fearfully this time, as the memory of the dreadful Shark came flooding back to her!

As Nattisa looked, she thought to herself, how cloudy the sea had become, as if some great current had swirled up, and disturbed all the sand from the sea floor, but, as her eyes got used to the gloom, where the sea was slowly clearing, she spotted the bodies lying on the sea floor, already the fishes were gathered round them, picking away at the dead flesh, and having a right horrible feast, at the expense of her friend Blip.

Nattisa swam really fast, and angrily, at the fishes, scaring them away , from the dead body of her friend, she beat at them with her small fists, tears streaming down her cheeks, the fishes had always been her friends, but, not today, today they were trying to eat her best friend, and Nattisa wasn't having that, not even if he was, dead, she wasn't going to let them do that, get away you horrid things, she said to the fishes, as she wept for her friend Blip, oh Blip, why did you have to go and get yourself killed, why did you not swim away when you had the chance to, did you do this for me, my friend, she said, why, oh why, I am not worthy of that, and I never even got a chance, to say Goodbye!!

Nattisa knelt down beside her dear friend, she put her arms around his neck, and hugged him close to her, then she said, her last goodbyes to him, and started to dig a hole in the sand near to where he lay, while all the time trying to keep the fishes away , from his poor dead body, they were determined to eat him, and she was determined, that they wouldn't, when she had dug a hole big enough and wide enough, she dragged and pushed her friend Blip, gently into the hole, and covered him over with sand, she then put small rocks and boulders, on top of him, and stuck seaweed in between the rocks, so that it looked like a natural foundation, of rocks and boulders, and no one would know that there was anything buried underneath, but Nattisa would know, and she would never forget her lifelong friend, who gave up his own life, to save hers!

It was a very sad young girl, who returned home that night, without her friend, to tell her parents the whole story, of what happened, to her and her Dolphin Blip, she was just eleven years old when, the incident with the Shark happened, but she would never forget it as long as she lived!!

The King and Queen, were very upset, about Nattisa's Dolphin friend, for they too, had thought a lot about Blip, but, they were more upset, that once again, Nattisa had put her life into danger, by straying too far, from the city.

What, if the Shark had killed you too, her Mother said, Nattisa, don't you realise yet, that you are the future of our race, and without you, we have no future, at all. Why then, do you persist in constantly, putting your life into danger, said her Mother, Nattisa replied, I've told you before Mother, I don't know, why, I do it, I just love to explore the sea, that's all, and I am never aware, that I am in any danger, until it is almost upon me, but, if it will make you feel any better, then I will promise that after this incident, I will not go too far from the city again!

Yes, her Mother said, it would make both myself and your father, feel much better, to know that you are safe, and that you are not, always, putting your life into danger, , with your careless ramblings away from home, but Mother, Nattisa said, I don't put my life into danger, on purpose, I've told you, I never know that I'm in danger, until it's almost too late, I mean no one ever, deliberately, put's their life in danger, do they, what pleasure would that give me, to know, that you worry about me constantly!

Exactly, her Mother replied, what would it pleasure you to know that, but, we do worry for you all the time, we know, that you don't do it on purpose, and maybe, you don't, know that you're in danger until it's nearly too late, but, one day it will be too late, one day, you may not, come home, to tell us a sad tale, because, one day you may be unable, to ever come home again, even so, I must admit, that I do feel better, now that you have made a promise, not to stray too far from the city again, the Queen then finished her lecture off, by giving her daughter a hug and a kiss, to show that she wasn't really angry with Nattisa, just concerned for her daughter's safety!

Come along now, the Queen said, let us stop arguing', come and show us the spot where, you buried your friend Blip, so that we can pay our last respect to him, and we will get the stone Mason, to make a headstone for his grave, so that all, who should come across the grave, will know what a brave Dolphin lies within, and they will know how that Dolphin, gave his own life, to save his friend, and future ruler, of the City! Queen Corali, was as good, as her word, there was a great gathering around Blip's grave, and the whole city, came to pay their last respects, to the creature, who had died to save their Princess, from certain death, at the hands of the Shark. Each and every person, turned and spat, on what was left of the Shark, who had dared, to attack their Princess, and had killed her friend Blip.

The people of Coral City, would all too soon forget this, they would even forget, where the Dolphin was buried, for Sea Sprites had short memories, but Nattisa would never forget, she may not grieve, as much for him in the future, as she did now, but, she would remember him always, and he would live in her heart, forever!!

CHAPTER THREE

THE PLAGUE

Time passed by, and the years rolled on quickly, Nattisa was growing into a very beautiful young woman, she made many new friends, but, she never forgot Blip, she would often refer back to the past, when she and Blip, had roamed the sea together, her new friends sometimes got bored with her tales, but, they never dared to tell her so, for fear of offending her, she was such a beautiful person, who had grown up into a sweet , gentle, caring and polite, young woman, as well as, being their Princess, and they would never dream of hurting her, by telling her that tales of the past, were boring them silly!

Nattisa had quite a few boyfriends, but, nothing serious, even though, her closest friend Marnie, was engaged to be married, Nattisa had no such plans, for herself, not yet anyway, for after all, she was only Fifteen years old, and there would be plenty of time for that later, when she found someone, who she could care enough, about to spend the rest of her life with, and she hadn't found that someone yet!

She was out swimming one day, but, only near the city, for she hadn't strayed far from home, not since the day that she had made the promise to her Mother, not since the Shark incident, especially near the area, where Blip had been killed, not even to visit his grave, and she was a little ashamed of that, but she had to keep her promise, to her mother, not to go too far away from the limits of Coral City!

Nattisa was floating gently on her back, just resting in the water, after a vigorous swim, when she noticed a strange looking plant, it was growing out of the rocks, and it was a plant, that she had never seen before, Nattisa had thought that she knew every plant and animal in the sea, how strange, she said to herself, to think that this plant , has been

19

growing so close to the city walls, and I have never noticed it before, it really was very odd indeed, for not much escaped the interest of Nattisa! She reached out to take hold of one of the plant's leaves, so that she could examine it in more detail, but, as her fingers touched the plant, she felt a searing pain shooting up her arm from her finger tips, and it was real agony!!

Nattisa cried out in pain, she let go of the plant, and dropped to her knees, the pain was so great in her fingers and arm, the whole of her arm felt as if it were on fire, the pain was scorching, and burning her so!!

She swam slowly back to the city, and had just reached the caves on the outskirts, when she collapsed in sheer agony, the last thing that she saw, was the boy that found her lying on the ground, for weeks after, Nattisa was so ill, she was burning up with fever, and was delirious, in and out of a faint, and all the time muttering and moaning.

The King and Queen had gathered from Nattisa's ramblings that it was a plant that had caused this fever in her, so they instructed the people to go out and collect some of this plant so that the Doctor could examine it and find out if he could make an antidote to the poison, he warned the people to wear protective clothing when collecting the plant so that they too would not get stung by the unknown plant as it had stung Nattisa ...

The Sprites searched everywhere, but, all they found was a brown withered thing that may have been the plant that they were looking for, no one could tell for there were no more strange plants in the area where they were searching and this was where they had been told to search, so apparently the plant must have died after injecting it's poison into the Princess, they returned to the city with empty hands and heavy hearts, once again they were afraid that they would lose their future Queen and ruler of Coral City.

The people wailed and moaned all the way back to the city, already they were grieving the loss of their Princess and future ruler, " oh what is to become of us they wailed, " who will look after us now that our Princess is dying, for our King and Queen are no longer in the prime of their youth and who knows how long they will survive after the death of their only daughter, that is if they do not follow her straight away from a broken heart! After all she had been their one and only child and they had loved her dearly, already the selfish people were talking of Nattisa in the past tense, they had given her up for dead and her parents along with her as well, for the Sprites, did not have a lot of faith in their Doctor to find a cure to the plants poison and make Nattisa well again ....

The people came up to the walls of the palace, but, out of hearshot of their rulers, they told the Doctor that the plant was dead and that they couldn't find any others like it. " If the plant is dead, they said to the Doctor, then how will you find a cure for what ails our Princess, shall we make burial arrangements for our sweet dead ruler, " what then will become of us they moaned, surely her parents will follow her, dead from a broken heart weighed down with such great sorrow at the death of their Daughter....

"Why you selfish load of hypocrites," the Doctor said angrily, "how dare you put such a death on our Princess and such a sorrow for that dying onto her parents, " you need not worry for yourselves, for even as you searched for the plant and even as we speak now, she is getting better with every minute that passes, " yes it is true, said the Doctor, she was very ill and I too feared that she may die, I cannot say why she is recovering, but, she is, already Nattisa has eaten and drank a little, I cannot say how soon she will be completely well again, but, she is well on the way now and if you wish to see her, you may do so later when she is recovered a bit more, " now go and repent your ways, he said, we shall not mention your selfishness again, I only hope that our rulers never get to hear about it for it would upset them so to know that their people were so selfish, as to only worry about themselves, so the Sprites left with their heads bowed low in shame, but, that would not last long for they were still selfish people, after all !!

As each day passed over Nattisa got better and better until she was completely recovered from the plants poison, to see her now no one would have guessed that just a few short weeks ago she was so ill, that all her people had given her up for dead....

She was a hundred percent better and looking all the more beautiful for it, all the young men of the city, the ones who had been in the crowd of people who had given her up for dead, they gave her no chance to survive her ordeal with the poison plant!! " Now these same men looked slyly at her with love and lust in their eyes and each one hoped that Nattisa would look to them when she was ready to find a mate, all the young maidens of the city were jealous of her, for they too wanted the men to look at them when they passed by, in the same way that they looked at Nattisa...

"But, Nattisa never noticed the lusty looks of the young men any more than she noticed the jealous looks of the maidens, she wanted no part of that, not now or ever, the men of her race had never really interested her in that way and probably never would, though why she just couldn't say and she had begun to think that there was something wrong with her, "I think that I will go and consult the Sea Witch, Nattisa said to herself, perhaps she can tell me why I don't care for the men of my race and she may be able to tell me if perhaps there is something wrong with me that I don't like men !!

I won't tell my parents where I am going, she thought to herself, after all I'm not going far and I won't be gone long, I'll be there and back without them even knowing where I've been, at least that is how she planned it, but, it didn't work out like that at all, for they did find out where she had been because she told them herself!

Nattisa arrived at the cave of the Witch just a couple of hours after leaving home, she swam quietly up to the entrance and knocked gently on the doorway, " come in," said a voice, from deep inside the cave, " I have been expecting you!

"But, how could you be expecting me, said Nattisa, I only knew myself just two hours ago that I would come to consult with you, "no," said the Witch, "I knew much longer than that, the rune stones that tell the future told me that you were coming to see me and the stones never lie, for here you are, now what can I do for you!!

"Well," replied Nattisa, my name is Nattisa and I am the Princess of the Sea Sprites who live in Coral City, " I know who you are and also what you are little Princess, I have followed your activities with much great interest, now tell me how can I assist you... Nattisa then nervously told the Witch why she had come to pay her a visit, she told of having no interest in the men of her race and finished off by asking the Witch if there was something wrong with her, because she didn't like men.

The Witch laughed and said, "no my little Princess there is nothing wrong with you," "I told your parents when they first came to ask me about you, that you were not for this race and that you were meant for a greater purpose, much greater than marrying a young man from the race of Sea Sprites or ruling over their city!!

The Witch then went on to tell Nattisa all about the night that her parents had come to ask about the baby that they were expecting, she told Nattisa everything that had been said between them," you were not even born when they came to see me, said the Witch, but, I thought that they would have told you by now, just what was said on the night of the visit, " no," replied Nattisa, they have told me nothing of what went on that night! "I wonder why, if they had told me what transpired that night then it may have answered a lot of my questions as to why I always wanted to explore the sea, instead of staying home safe and why I always felt different to my race, besides the difference between us of being their Princess, " I have never really felt as if I am one of them!!

"Yes," said the Witch, they were wrong to try to stop you from exploring and wrong to try and keep you at home, you have to learn to know yourself and then you can find out who you really are, but, perhaps that is why they tried to keep you home so much, maybe they were trying to prevent you from finding out too much about yourself, because they didn't want to lose you, being their only child you mustn't blame them too much for that. They tried to wrap you up and protect you, but, they do really love you," perhaps they tried to wrap you up to protect you from yourself, " when you were younger you really were a danger to yourself and could have been killed more than once if it had not been for your parents protecting you God knows what might have happened....

"But, I really think that it's time that they let you go now don't you, so that you can find your true self and maybe then we shall learn what the future has in store for you! "All that you tell me I know to be true, said Nattisa, but, do you really think that my parents will listen to me and let me go my own way, "No," said the Witch, but, maybe they will listen to me or both of us together, for I am quite prepared to go with you to talk to them on your behalf, so shall we go to the city together and face them as one... The odd-looking pair then set off for Coral City together, one beautiful young Girl of Fifteen and a half years old and one withered ugly old crone of lord knows how many years old, " too old to count on the fingers of all the people of the city, but, they were a determined pair and would not be easily swayed from the task before them.

They entered the city walls together and proudly they made their way towards the palace, the people of the city all stopped what they were doing and stared at the odd couple who were walking down the main street towards the palace, " their Princess walking side by side with the ancient Sea Witch, " what is she up to now, they asked each other? " But, they still bowed down their heads in respect of the pair passing by them proudly with their heads held high, the people bowed firstly in respect of their Princess and secondly in respect of the Witch because they feared her, but, it didn't stop them from wondering what these two were doing together and just what the Witch wanted in the city!!

Nattisa and the Witch finally reached the palace complete with a large following of nosey people all wanting to know what was going on, " when it was really none of their concern at all, but, that didn't stop them from wanting to know anyway....

The odd pair entered the palace portals and from this point on the people were not able to follow, the palace Guards barred their way and would not let them pass, no matter how nosey they were or how angrily they muttered they were not allowed in, so they had to content themselves with hanging around outside, straining and hoping to hear a bit of news from their nearest neighbour to get the smallest notion of what was happening... The nosey Sprites chattered together noisily each asking the other did they know what was going on in the palace and all annoyed that no one knew anything at all!

"What big trouble is our Princess involved in now," one Sprite said to her friend at her side, "I don't know replied her friend, but, it must be Big trouble to involve the Sea Witch, "Oh if only someone would tell us just what is going on, they cried: The first Sprite who had spoken, said to her friend, " our Princess is always getting into trouble of one kind or another, "why the first time that I saw her when she was just a babe in arms, I knew then that she would be a trouble both to us and to her parents, "why I distinctly remember telling everyone to look out for her and that she would be a real handful when she was growing up, now everyone will see just how right I was in my judgement of her, this was the same Sprite who had said that Nattisa looked like a real Angel on the first day that she was presented before her people !!

The palace Guards who were getting rather annoyed because of all the muttering and jawing that was going on outside of the palace, tried their best to get the noisy Sprites to go away, "Be off with you," one of the guards said to the people, " you are making far too much of a disturbance and you will make the King and Queen very angry both with you and with us for not moving you on, but, the nosey people were afraid of missing out on something no matter how much it made the Royal couple angry...

So they compromised, they wouldn't go away altogether, but, they did drop back by about twenty feet or so, they were afraid to let the Guards hear what they were saying anyway as it was treason to talk like that, about any member of the Royal Family, much less their future ruler and even though they couldn't stop from saying it, they didn't want to be heard saying it or even seen by the Guards, so when speaking they hid their faces. The Guards who were stationed by the door inside of the palace, stood by the Royal Chambers and they were rather surprised to see the Witch side by side with Nattisa, but, when the Princess informed them that she and the Witch sought an audience with the King and Queen, the Guards ushered them inside without hesitation!

It was more than their job was worth to refuse their Princess and one and only child of the Royal couple an audience with her own parents, "it did not matter who was by her side they would never dream of trying to prevent her from entering the Royal Chamber.

Nattisa approached her parents, who were seated together, talking about matters concerning the running of the city, they looked up as their daughter approached them, and smiled at her warmly, till they saw who was behind her, then the smiles, stiffened on their faces, and froze there, and in their eyes was so much, sadness and fear.

Good day, Mother and Father, said Nattisa, I trust that you are feeling well, this day, both of you, because I wish to tell you, that, I went to visit with someone today, I went because, I needed some advice, on a subject of some importance to me, but, I got a lot more than advice from this person, I got a whole lot of information too!

I would like to introduce you to the Sea Witch, but, I think that, you already know her, don't you, she, has told me a very interesting story, about a couple, who came to consult her, about a baby, that they were expecting, at the time.

She gave this couple much information, about their expected child, but, I think that, it was information that, they didn't understand, or didn't want to believe, so they thought that, because they, didn't believe in this information, that they would not pass on to their child, when she was old enough, to understand, just what had been told to them, on the night in question, so this couple, thought, that they would keep it to themselves. Instead they must have thought, that, if they wrapped the child up, then they could protect it, from learning all about it's own future, and if they kept the child to them, and stopped it from exploring, and trying to find itself, that it would never leave them, and that what they had been told, about their child's future, would never really happen. But, you cannot, shut your eyes to the future, what is to happen, will happen, and nothing that, you or I, can do, will change that, and speaking as the child who was denied the knowledge, of it's future, the child that, you tried to protect and smother, I ask you my parents, who I love and trusted, above all others, why did you not tell me, what was told to you on that night, and why did you try to keep me from my future!!

Her parents looked at her, and there was so much sadness in their eyes, Nattisa, her Mother said, we did not try to keep you from your future on purpose, for one thing, half the time we forgot, and when we did remember, we didn't understand it.

We thought that the Witch meant, that you were going to be a murderer, and that you would be responsible for the death of all your people, including us, we were trying to protect both you, and the people of the city, from this thing taking place.

The Witch looked at the sad defeated couple, I do not remember saying anything, about your daughter being a murderer, she said, you really must have misunderstood what I was saying. My exact words were, that your daughter was to be the beginning, for a new race of people and she could only do that, at the cost of our people, I could not tell you any more at the time, because I didn't know any more, not then anyway, but, I did not mention a thing about her being a Killer of men, you must have been hearing more from my words, than what I was actually saying, either that or you weren't listening properly!

I have since consulted the rune stones, the Witch said, they tell me over, and over, that the Princess is to be the Mother of a new race, they do not tell me how, or why, but, they do predict that our race must die, to make way for the new race.

This does not mean, that we are going to die at the hands of your daughter, it means that, out of all the race of Sprites, she will be the only one to survive, the stones do not say, how, our race will be destroyed, only that they must be, and if you are truthful with yourselves, you will admit, that our people are not much use here on Middle Earth! They are a stupid childish people, who even now as we speak, are gathered outside the palace, dying to know what is going on, they are mean, selfish, petty like children, stubborn and downright useless, the only thing they are concerned about is, how they feel, how beautiful they are, and if their stomachs are full.

All this the Witch told them, then she said, if we are to go forward in this world instead of going backwards, or standing still, then the race of Sprites must be sacrificed, to make way for a more intelligent, caring race, of whom your daughter is to be the beginning of, according to the rune stones, and they do not lie! Then the Witch rested!!

When is all this to happen, the Queen said, when will our people die, how long have we got, the Witch looked sadly at the Queen, I have told you that I don't know this, said the Witch, and I would not lie to you, all I do know, is that this prophecy includes all our people, even you and the King, and also myself, even I cannot escape from this fate!

The King who had listened patiently to all this information, suddenly spoke, if all this is true, he said, then I suggest that we make up our quarrels, let our daughter go out to explore and find her future, and make the most of our last times together, then he held out his arms to encircle his family within them, and to the Witch he gave a warm friendly smile, and told her, that she would be welcome at the palace, any time.

I will inform the guards, he said, that you must be allowed in or out of the palace, any time you choose to visit, whether it be day or night, thank you for your kindness, the Witch said, but, that will not be necessary, for even though your offer is much appreciated I won't be coming here again, time is short, and if I am to die soon, then I have a lot to do, I must get all my affairs in order, to make way for my replacement.

I know that it won't be for years before someone comes to take my place, but, come she will, and if my affairs are in well enough order, then she will know what to do, and just what is expected of her, maybe in another Fifty years or so, there will be another Witch, who will be almost, but, not quite as good as I am now!

So saying, the Witch rose to go, she bowed with deep respect to the Royal Family, said her goodbyes and left the Royal Chamber, and they never saw her again!

After the Witch had gone, Nattisa and her parents tried to make their peace together, I am so sorry, said Nattisa, I had no right to speak to you the way I did earlier on, I spoke so angrily and without respect, will you ever be able to forgive me.

The Queen said, yes we can forgive you, you had every right to speak to us in that way, for you were angry that we were keeping things from you, things that concerned your future, you had a right to know these things, and we were wrong to try to keep them from you, I cannot speak for your Father, but, I am very sorry for not telling you, what the Witch told us on the night that we visited her, all those years ago!

I think that it's time we forget all about that, said the King, it's out in the open now, so let us try to get on with the time that we have left, instead of always dwelling on the past, we should go forward to the future now, at least what's left of it.

Now I think that it's time, to go out and make up a story to tell our people, for we don't want them starting a panic, which is what they will do, if they learn the truth. So the Royal Family went out united, to tell the people some story about the Princess, going to consult the Witch on a matter of someone who she was in love with, she wanted a love potion from the Witch, so that this person would fall in love with her too.

Having been satisfied with what was going on, and believing in the word of their Rulers, the people began to disperse, and drifted slowly back to their own homes, each one saying to the other, see I told you that it was nothing to worry about, and each young man hoping desperately, that it was he, who the Princess was in love with:

It was a few months after this incident, that the first of the people, went to the city Doctor complaining of feeling very ill, the Doctor gave the woman a thorough examination, and took some of her blood for testing, he gave her some medicine that he had extracted from a clump of seaweed, well known for it's healing properties, and the woman went away being assured that within a few days, she would be well again.

The Doctor examined the sample of blood, that he had taken from the woman, in it he found an active germ, that he had never encountered before, he tried several different cures on this germ, including the one he had given to the woman, but, nothing worked.

The germ just got stronger and stronger, in fact it seemed to thrive on all the cures that he fed to it, nothing could kill it, and he didn't know what it was, a few days after he had tried everything he knew to kill the germ, with no success, he decided to go to see the woman in her own cave, to see how she was, he knocked on the entrance to the cave, it brought the woman's husband to the door, the Doctor noticed right away that the man looked drawn and weary, as if from lack of sleep, I have come to enquire how your wife is, the Doctor said, I am glad of that, replied the man, for I was going to come to see you about her anyway, please come in, said the man, I would like you to take a look at her, for she has kept me up these last few nights, the cure that you gave her did not work, in fact I fear that she is worse, and I am at my wits end as to know what to do for her.

The Doctor entered the cave of the sick woman, followed silently behind by her weary husband, it took him a while for his eyes to get used to the gloom of the cave, but, when they had, this is what he saw, at the back of the cave lay the woman, she was lying on a low flat rock platform that served as a bed, the platform was covered in a soft layer of fresh green seaweed, which made the woman look very pale lying on it, her face was white as the foam on the crest of the waves, and her hair was matted with dried up vomit, on her face and hands were great sores, all yellow and festering, these had come up in just the few days, since she had been to see the Doctor!

He looked down on this woman who had been to see him first only days ago, and he couldn't believe that it was the same woman, she looked awful, and she had aged about Ten years since he saw her only days before, he stared at the pitiful sight before him, and he was afraid, very afraid, he was dealing with some disease here, that he knew nothing about, and it made him frightened, both for the woman, and her husband if it was catching, but, mostly he was afraid for himself, he was a Doctor second, but, he was a Sprite first, and being a Sprite meant that he was no different from the other Selfish Sprites, who always put number one first, he mumbled something to the man, about hoping that his wife would soon be better, and he backed out of the cave with fear in his eyes, as he darted out of the cave, he told the man that he would send some new cure for his wife, but, he had no intention of coming back to see the woman, not till he could find a cure, for himself!!

He went back to his surgery cave, determined to find a cure for the unknown germ, but, to protect himself, just in case he should catch this germ, after all, he said to himself, if I was to catch this germ, what would my people do without me to cure them, he knew that he was only making excuses to himself, to cover up for his selfishness, he knew that he was going to hide himself away, so that he would not have to come into contact with any more sick people, and he was sure that there would be more cases of this germ turning up, for if his suspicion of what the germ was, turned out to be correct, then the people of Coral City were going to have a right plague on their hands, he didn't know yet if it was a killer plague, because he had never encountered one before, but, he rather suspected that it was a killer, and he had no intention of being one of it's victims, he intended to keep well away from the rest of the people, till all this was over!

And he did just that, over the next few weeks, more and more people came to see him to complain of feeling unwell, including the woman's husband, to ask for help for his wife, but, the Doctor refused to see any of them, and turned them all away from his door, after all he said, excusing himself again, I know of no cure for them yet, perhaps there is no cure, so what use would it be for me to endanger myself, by seeing these sick people, who I probably can't help anyway, I'll be far better off working indoors, trying to find a cure to help these people, by scientific means, so saying this he stayed within the walls of his cave, while all around him outside, his people were sick and slowly dying from the plague, because their one and only Doctor had turned his back on them, and cared only to find a cure to save himself from their affliction!

CHAPTER FOUR

THE PEOPLE ARE DYING

The woman who was the first patient, that the Doctor had tried to treat, was dying slowly and painfully in front of her helpless husband, he had to stand by and watch, as the once beautiful flesh withered and dropped off her.

He stood by, not knowing what to do for her, she was screaming in agony, her hair had fallen out of her head by the handful, she had lost all her teeth, and her flesh and bones were just rotting away, right in front of his eyes!

The great sores had grown so large, and the festering had joined them together, thus spreading them all over her face and body, where they met great holes had formed in the skin, holes that oozed with yellow and green puss, the skin underneath her eyes had sagged with the weight of these sores, and one of the eyes just hung there, on what was left of her cheek bone, it was just hanging by the finest thread, to the eye sockets Her husband looked at this quivering lump before him, it was hard for him to believe, that this thing, used to be the wife that he loved, it bore no resemblance to her at all any more, suddenly, his will broke, and he fled from the cave in terror.

But, even as he ran, he knew that he would soon be joining her, for already the sores were forming on his hands and face, and the thought of that terrified him even more! When he finally stopped running, he sat down on a large rock to catch his breath, and started to think, if I already have the sores, he thought, then it will not be long, before I begin to look like my wife does now, and the prospect of that did not thrill him at all, no, he thought, I have no wish to look like the horrible mess, that I left back there in the cave, that used to be my happy home, before my wife became ill.

I do not wish to die like that, in so much pain with no one to turn to for help, and as these thoughts were running through his mind, he picked a large mussel shell, and cut his throat, slashing at his jugular vein till the blood spurted out!!

Then he slashed at his wrists, and as he slowly died, the life force draining out of him, he had the satisfaction of knowing that he was dying how he wanted to, peacefully just like going to sleep, but, with dignity, not the way his poor wife was dying, wasn't that just like a Sprite, selfish to the end!!

The people were going down like flies now, the streets of the city were littered with the bodies of the dead and dying, it hit some people harder and faster than others, and it was a horrible sight to see all those mutilated bodies, that had once been beautiful people, the King and Queen, and Nattisa, were doing their best to help them, but, without medicine, there was not a lot they could do!

We must go to see the Doctor, the King said, he cannot stay in his cave while our people are suffering so, we must order him to come out and treat them, I know that he can't cure them, for this must be the prophecy coming true, but, at least he can give them something to ease their pain, if he only gives us some medicine for them, it would be better than him doing nothing at all, surely he can't refuse us that.

So they set out for the Doctor's cave, all along the way they saw people so ill, that they could not even manage to get back to their homes, and the Royal Family felt so helpless, because there was nothing that they could do.

They arrived at the cave shortly before noon, and knocked on the entrance, for even though none of the caves in Coral City had any doors, it was not manners to enter without first knocking, they waited for a while, but, when no answer came from inside the cave, they knocked again, only this time louder and longer than before.

A small feeble voice came from inside of the cave, who is it that seeks entrance here, said the voice, it is I your King, said the King, I have with me the Queen, and the Royal Princess, and we demand that you collect together all your cures, and come out of your cave onto the streets of the city, to try and help the suffering people. The voice from inside said, I am sorry my King, but, I cannot do that, I cannot come out onto the city streets, but, you are more than welcome, to come in and help yourselves to any of the cures, that you think might help the people.

The King grew angry then, damn you man, he said, do not be such a selfish coward, his voice roared into the cave entrance, what is the matter with you, are you so afraid to catch the plague, why then did you become a Doctor and take an oath to always help our people, no matter what was wrong with them!

No my King, said the feeble voice, which was getting harder to hear every time it spoke, I am no longer afraid to catch the plague, the voice said, but, I still cannot come out to you, for I am unable to walk, as I already have the plague, there is nothing that I can do for the people, because, I can't even do it for myself!

When they heard this, the Royal Family just looked at each other, that was when they knew there was nothing more to hope for, the rune stone prophecy was coming true, they gathered together all their courage and entered the cave of the Doctor!!

As they slowly came into the depth of the cave, it took a while for their eyes to get used to the gloom, but, when their eyes had adjusted, and could see better, this is what they saw in the dingy looking cave, that the Doctor called home.

All around the walls were shelves full of bottles, in all shapes and sizes, and on the large rock that served as a table, there stood funny looking equipment for doing all the different operations, such as teeth pulling for one, over in the corner of the cave on the floor, was what at first sight appeared to be a bundle of rags.

As the Queen looked more closely at the bundle of rags, it appeared to move, oh, the Queen exclaimed, it moved, the rags moved, did you see them, and sure enough, Nattisa and her father had seen the bundle of rags definitely move.

They went closer to have a better look at the bundle of rags, and wished that they hadn't, for it turned out to be a bundle of flesh and bone, or at least what was left of it, the creature squatting in the corner of the cave was horrific!!

It had no eyes for they had completely rotted away, the place where the nose had been was just a gaping hole, it had no teeth, in fact it didn't even have gums, and the lower jaw of the creature just hung down, onto what had once been it's chest, but, was now just a sunken cavity, with the breast bones protruding through!

How the creature had managed to speak to them, when they were stood outside it's cave, they would never know, for the bones that held the jaw onto the head were rotted away too. The feet of the creature were no where to be seen, neither were it's legs, all that was left of them was a load of quivering mess of blood and gore, only the knees were left, and they too were rotting away fast, and would soon be gone!

The Queen tried not to look at this thing pulsating in the corner, but, she couldn't help herself, she kept thinking that just a short while ago, this creature used to be their Doctor, who had selfishly shut himself up in his cave, in order to save himself from the plague, what good had that done him, why looking at what was left of him now, it had done him no good at all, no good whatsoever, and if he couldn't save himself from dying, then what chance had anyone else, including them.

The King slowly raised his hard coral spear, and struck the thing straight through the heart, putting it out of it's misery, he did wrong to lock himself away from the plague, and not try to help the people, said the King, but, I think that he had suffered enough don't you, now he can at last rest in peace, if there is such a thing!

After the Doctor had been helped out of this world, the King sent for a couple of the palace guards, who he employed in helping him to dispose of the Doctor's body, or at least what was left of it, the guards did not relish this gruesome task, but, they knew that they dare not refuse, as it was a direct order from their King, and besides that, he was helping them in the distasteful job, he did not expect them to do it alone.

When the task was completed and the gruesome remains laid to rest, the King ordered the guards to go and get the rest of their comrades, and to assemble in the main street of the city, to then dispose of any dead bodies that they should find there.

He explained that by doing this, perhaps the plague germ would be buried along with the dead people, and there would be less chance of the rest of them catching it!

The guards looked at their King, and they were horrified at his words, their eyes were filled with fear and their faces were white as snow.

To think that the King could give them such an order, as to endanger their lives, the poor terrified men were having none of this, they left as if to do the King's bidding, but, as soon as they got out into the street, the guards fled for their very lives! They looked at the dead and dying people around them, and said to each other, damn the people let them bury themselves, we must get right away from this cursed city, if we are to save ourselves, and so saying that is exactly what they did do, kept on going forever.

The King spent his time, while waiting for the guards to return, in disposing of all the bottles and equipment in the Doctor's cave, hoping that this would help to slow down the fast-spreading plague, though he knew it was a waste of time.

He smashed and buried everything that was in there, till the whole cave was swept completely clean and bare, he knew that it would do no good, but, he had to try. After a good while had passed, the King began to wonder just what had happened to the guards, and why they were taking so long, they should have been there and back by now, he thought to himself, perhaps I had better go and look for them.

So thinking this, he set off for the palace, it took him quite a while to get there, as all along the way he had to keep stopping to give comfort to the sick, and his blessing to the dead, the poor people who were dragging themselves through the streets, held up their arms to him as he passed them by, but, there was nothing that he could do for them. The main street to the palace was littered with the bodies of the sick and dead, they had all tried to reach the palace, to ask for help from the Royal Family, and had died before they could reach even the palace walls!

The King had to step over them every few yards or so, and they were so thick on the ground that he kept stumbling over them, that's when he decided to give up trying to walk, and thought to himself, I must swim for it, if I am ever to get home.

When he finally reached the palace, he was so fatigued from the short journey, that he collapsed into the nearest shell chair to get his breath back, it took him some time to recover, he was so weak and weary from fighting his way up the main street to his home, but, he was just coming round when the Queen and Nattisa entered the room, to find out what was going on, for they were afraid to go out for fear of the people! Have you seen the main street to the palace, the King asked them, yes they said, the poor people have been trying to reach the palace all morning, they must have thought that there was something that we could do to save them, though I don't know what.

I wish we could have helped them, said Nattisa, but, we are as helpless against this plague as they are, I know that the Sprite race has to be destroyed, to make way for the new race, she said, but, did the fates have to choose such an horrible and cruel way to dispose of them, they were such beautiful people, and the fates are cruel indeed to kill them, and also rob them of that beauty, that they were so proud of!

The Queen said, I know, I feel so sorry for my people too, because I am one of them, and I know that your Father and I are going to go the same way as them, but, thank the Gods that you, our one and only daughter will be spared this fate too.

Now, we must get the guards of the palace, to make a burial detail to dispose of the bodies properly, so that the plague will not spread quite so quickly.

That is the reason, why I came back to the palace, said the King, I told the guards who. were with me at the Doctor's cave, to come to the palace and organise a burial detail with the other guards, but, that was some hours ago now, and they have not returned, I fear that something awful must have happened to them!!

The Queen and Nattisa, were alarmed when they heard this, we must set out to find them, said the Queen, tell us who we are looking for and we shall get the other guards to join in the search for them, now what are their names.

The King told them the names of the missing guards, and each of them set off in different directions, to warn the other guards to look out for the missing men, and they arranged that all of them should meet up again in the centre courtyard, bringing with them the rest of the guards, so that the King could tell them what was required of them! The King went off to search the left half of the palace for the guards, while the Queen and Nattisa searched the right half, they knew that it would take some time to find anyone, as the palace was so huge in all it's splendour.

It had been built hundreds of years ago by their ancestors, the inside was made up of several large caves joined together by holes, that had been knocked through from one cave to another, so that they were like adjoining rooms.

The outside had been made from layer upon layer, of gorgeous coloured shells and coral, there were colours of Pink, White, Red, Yellow and a beautiful Salmon colour, it looked like a rainbow, but, with much softer colours, and when the sun shone down into the depths of the sea, from the outside world, as soon as it hit the palace with it's rays, the whole beautiful structure shimmered and sparkled, like some heavenly vision, this building was their pride and joy, and they loved it, it was their Home!

The inside was absolutely massive, it had taken so many caves to make up the interior, that it was like a maze, and it took them ages to search the width and length of the magnificent building, but, they finally made it through, and went to meet up in the courtyard, as previously arranged.

The Queen and Nattisa arrived first, looking rather puzzled, as they had searched high and low, and found not one person in the place at all, even the maids were noticeable by their absence, heaven knows where everyone had disappeared to!

The King arrived shortly after, and he too had been unable to find anyone either, "it appears that we have been deserted my dear" he said to his wife, the entire company of guards have gone, perhaps to be with their wives and families in their hour of need, or maybe they have just fled to save themselves!!

"I know replied his wife, the Queen, " even the maids and the rest of the staff have disappeared and we are left alone, to deal with the plague, the best that we can, such loyalty to their King and Queen, and to the Royal Princess is overwhelming!!

They were very annoyed at having been deserted by the staff and guards, but, in these times of crisis there wasn't much that they could do about it, there was not time to go out and look for the runaway people, and the King was more annoyed, that there was no one to help in burying the dead, who were littering the streets of the city, he knew that he could not perform the task alone, and he would not dare to ask the Queen and Nattisa for help, besides which there were more and more people arriving all the time!

The King told his wife and daughter what was bothering him, and Nattisa remembering how the fishes had tried to eat her dead friend Blip, said to her father, perhaps the Fish will eat the dead bodies and take the plague with them.

I doubt that very much, replied the King, if you will take notice, you will see that the Fish are keeping well away from the bodies, I think that they sense that the people did not die of natural causes, Nattisa looked around, and she saw that her father was right, there was not one Fish to be seen anywhere, but, she had been so busy with the problem of the plague, that she hadn't time to notice the missing Fish!

Yes I can see that you are right Father, said Nattisa, I can see there are no Fish in sight at all, and the city is usually teeming with them, then what are we to do with the dead bodies , she said, the King replied, I fear that we must leave them where they are, for I doubt that we alone are up to the task of disposing of them all, or even half of them, they number too many, and more are arriving even now as we speak, I fear that we should die of exhaustion well before the plague claimed us, for the task is too great to contemplate even trying to start it, and I don't see any way round the problem. Even so the thought that every time they looked through the palace windows, they would see all the bodies of the dead and dying people, did not go down too well with them at all, so although they loved their Home, they knew that if they were to get any peace at all, then they must up stakes and find somewhere else to live, for the short time that they had together, before the plague claimed them too!!

So they got together the few things that could be easily carried, and left the place that had been their home for as long, as they could remember, and leaving the Palace they went on their way and never looked back, for their hearts were breaking inside them. Where are we to go, said the Queen, to her husband and daughter, she stepped over the bodies of the people, all the time wanting to be sick and trying not to look down at them, suddenly with the weight of the belongings that she was carrying, and trying not to look down, she stumbled over someone's legs and landed right on top of a man, with the top half of his body and face completely rotted away!

Queen Corali took one look at this pathetic creature that she had landed on, and she started to scream, on and on she went, unable to stop herself, Nattisa and her Father tried to calm the Queen down, they tried reasoning with her, with no results, then they shook her roughly and finally the King gave her a real hard slap across the face, till she finally stopped and collapsed into his arms, sobbing her heart out, so weak, tired and exhausted, but, mostly afraid, firstly for what had become of the people all around her feet, and secondly for what was to become of herself.

Oh, my dearest one, she sobbed to the King, I cannot stand it anymore, I am not as strong and brave as you think I am, I cannot face the fact easily that I am going to die, and look like the rest of my people do now, I am weak and afraid, call me a coward if you must, but, I don't want to die or to look like that, she said, pointing down at the man that she had fallen on top of, and she started to cry again!

Don't worry, said Nattisa to both her parents, I will never let either of you look like that, and she too pointed at the man, you and Father go, and find one of the caves outside of the city, to rest and set up temporary home in, and I will go to see the Sea Witch to get a potion for you, the plague will not have reached her yet, as she is outside the city limits, and it will take the disease a while yet, to reach her!

I will obtain a sleeping potion from her, so that as soon as the sores start to appear on your skin, I can give you the potion and it will make you sleep, never to wake in this world again, but, at least you will have the satisfaction of knowing that you will both be going together, and that you will look as you do now, but, I will not tell you when I give the potion to you, so that you won't be frightened Mother!

Now let us all go about our business: as we have not much time, and when you have found a suitable cave for the three of us, then mark it with something, so that I will be able to find you easily, when I return from my visit with the Witch.

So they all kissed and went on their way, Nattisa to see the Witch, and her parents to find them all a temporary home, for the length of time that they would all be together! Nattisa stood watching, as the parents that she loved so much, carefully stepped over the bodies, of the people who had once been such a beautiful race, now they were nearly all gone, wiped out by a plague sent by the fates, because the Sprites had been too vain and selfish, and childish, to exist anymore, then how was she herself to be spared, if the plague was so contagious surely even, she wouldn't be spared either.

By the time she had arrived at the cave of the Witch, she had made up her mind to ask that very question of the Witch, Nattisa had hardly entered the cave properly, when she said to the Witch, why and how have I, to be the only one to survive the plague, if it is so contagious then surely, I shall catch it too!!

No, my Princess, replied the Witch, not surprised to see Nattisa at all, for the rune stones had told her of Nattisa's coming, I have already told you that you are to be spared, because you are to be the Mother of a new race!

Then, she said, I have told you why, you are to be spared, now I will tell you how, do you remember well before the time of the plague, you found a plant outside the city walls, you touched the strange plant and it stung you, do you remember that?

Yes I remember, said Nattisa, it nearly killed me, but, what has that plant to do with my not catching the plague, well use your brain my Princess, said the Witch, the poison that the plant injected into you was the antidote to the plague, that is how you are going to be saved from the plague, because through that strange plant injecting it's poison into you, you are now immune from the killer plague, that is how the fates have decreed it, and that is how it is going to be!!

So it was the sting of the strange plant that made me immune to the plague, said Nattisa, if that is correct, then I shall pick more of the plants to make cures for my Mother and Father, for you and whoever is left of our people.

I am sorry, but, that is not possible, said the Witch, though you do not know it, for you were unconscious at the time, the people of the city found the plant dead and withered after it had stung you, so you see there will be no more cures for anyone else. The Doctor had sent them to get a sample of the plant to examine, he wished to know more about it. so that he could make an antidote to save you from

43

it's poison, although you didn't really need a cure, he didn't know that at the time, anyway the plant is dead! Well then, I shall search for more plants of the same kind, said Nattisa, No replied the Witch, that will not work either, for there are no more of it's kind, it was the one and only in existence, you won't find another like it anywhere in this world.

If you were to search all the Seas and Oceans, you would never find another of that kind, don't you understand yet, my Princess, why do you think that you were the one to find the plant and no one else, it was not Mother Nature who put the plant there for you to find, it was the Gods who rule the Seas for they have decreed that you and only you, will survive the onslaught of this terrible plague.

And now let us get back to the reason why you came to see me, what can I do for you?" said the Witch,"I came to get a sleeping potion for my parents, said Nattisa, one that will make sure that they sleep well and peacefully and never wake up forever! No not forever, said the Witch, only in this life will they sleep, in the next world they go to live with the Gods of the sea, for your father is to become one of the greatest Gods ever, he will be given a new name, and that name will be Poiseiden!! Your Mother also will be given a new name and become a great Goddess of the sea, for all her grace and beauty and the depth of love that she has shown, she shall take the name Venus, and they both shall be ever immortal, and their names shall go down in history, and all who hear those names, shall bow before them.

After hearing all this, Nattisa felt much better, in fact better than she had done in days, much happier, and she knew that when it came time to say goodbye to her parents and to give them the potion, then she wouldn't feel quite so guilty about it! The Witch then gave Nattisa the brew that she had come for, and they hugged each other, said all their goodbyes, and then Nattisa left the cave of the Witch forever, the Princess left with a sad heart, because she knew that they would never see each other again, not in this world anyway, then she started off on her journey back to her parents

Nattisa had been swimming for a couple of hours towards the city, when she spotted a long bright Yellow cloak hanging from the side of a large cave, she knew this must be a sign from her parents, and that the cave must have been chosen to be their new home, for just a short time anyway, till she was left alone!

She swam towards the cave with such renewed energy, and happiness in her heart at the thought of seeing them again, even though it was only Five hours since last she saw them, Nattisa thought that her heart was going to burst with pleasure, although the moment did not last, for when she entered the cave and saw them both, the shock of the sight of them knocked the happiness right out of her and she went rigid with fear!!

They were both propped up together leaning on the wall of the cave for support, their faces were as white as a sheet and covered in the red sores, the sores were not very large at the moment, but, they were growing slowly.

Both of them opened their eyes with much effort to look at her, then closed them again exhausted by just that small movement, and Nattisa knew that their time was up! Oh no, she cried, not yet please, don't take them so soon, she prayed to the Gods, I thought that I would have a bit more time with them than this, I know that the damn plague strikes hard and fast, but, it's only five hours since I last saw them!

Please let me have a bit more time with them, don't please don't, take them quite so soon as this I beg you, she implored the Gods, but, she knew that it wasn't up to the Gods anymore, they had done their part in starting the plague, and now that her parents had caught it, she knew that it was now up to her to end their misery, because she had made them a promise, and that promise had to be kept, for their sake, not hers!!

So she knelt down beside them and tenderly holding first her Mother and then her father, she gave them both the whole bottle of sleeping mixture, and when it was all gone, she kissed them both goodbye, and then gently pressed them together, so that they went to their final sleep in each other's arms, she took one last look at them and left the cave and her parents forever, and dropping onto the sea floor she wept, like she had never wept before, great sobs racking through her heart broken body!!

When her tears had finally subsided, she went in search of one of her sea friends, Toby who was a killer whale, Nattisa brought him back with her to the cave and there he helped her to start a landslide of rocks, when the work was finally finished, the cave was completely covered for all time and the sleep of her parents would remain for all eternity undisturbed by any man or animal, be he good or evil!

And Nattisa left the bright Yellow cloak hanging from the outside of the cave as a reminder to herself just who was buried there, not that she would forget anyway...

CHAPTER FIVE

MACORMACK

For a long while after her parents had died, Nattisa hung around the cave feeling very sorry for herself, she would not eat, or go off exploring, she just sat on a rock outside the cave, looking wistfully at the blocked entrance, mourning her loss!

Her hair was a tangled mess which she hadn't combed for days now, and her face was so gaunt and thin, the cheeks were sunk in, and underneath her eyes were dark rings from lack of sleep, her once shapely figure was so thin from lack of food which she denied it. During those black sad days, Toby the whale came often to see her, he would come right up and tickle her with his nose, and he tupped Nattisa, and tugged at her trying to get her to join in the fun, looking for a response of some kind, but, he got none, she completely ignored him, Nattisa wasn't into playing yet, her grief was too raw at this moment in time, perhaps she would feel up to it later, but, not yet!

Weeks went by with her just eating enough to stay alive and neglecting her appearance, when suddenly she snapped out of her mood, enough is enough, she thought, if I am to be the Mother of a new race then I must pull myself together, I shall hence go forth to find my future mate, whoever he may be, how I go about that, only the Gods know!! The next time that Toby came around to play, Nattisa was feeling better still, so off she went with him to play and explore, but, first, she thought that she had better clean herself up a bit and have something to eat.

They swam off together and Nattisa found a coral comb, and began to untangle her long straggly blonde hair, it looked much better after she had given it a good combing, it hung around her shoulders and waist, the lovely glossy locks falling into curls, and apart from still being too thin, she began to look more like her normal self again! While she was busy combing her hair, Toby had been out collecting her some fish for her to eat, and with that, she had a few Oysters and Mussels, some sea urchins and a good helping of seaweed, after that scrumptious meal Nattisa felt a whole lot better than she had done in days now, but, she didn't look any better, not yet anyway.

After she had rested for a while to let her meal digest, she watched Toby swimming around her, he was chasing fish and tossing floating seaweed around with his nose, she watched him for quite some time, then got up and went to join in the fun, they played with the seaweed for a bit, then getting bored with that, they went off together to do some real exploring and have some adventures, which Nattisa hadn't done in quite a while!

They had been swimming for ages totally engrossed in all that they saw, when Nattisa realised that they were getting near to the city, she stood for a while looking at the forlorn ghost city, and at the beautiful palace that used to be her home, Toby wanted to explore further going right into the city itself, but, Nattisa wasn't ready for that yet, it was much too soon and there were too many raw memories!

She could still see in her mind the once beautiful people laughing and playing in the streets, then suddenly she could see again, their bodies rotting away to corpses and littering the streets to the palace, with unspeakable sights of horror!!

And that was when she forced her mind to call a halt to the pictures running through; it, then Nattisa turned her back on the cursed city and changed direction completely, maybe one day long into the future, she may go back to the city to look round or even to reclaim her home, one day perhaps when the corpses have long disappeared, but, not yet! Nattisa and Toby travelled far together over the next few months, she had lots of other friends among the sea creatures, but, Toby was her best one, that was until she met Macormack..., and he turned out to be her best friend of all!!

Toby had gone off to hunt fish as he was hungry, Nattisa was relaxing and teasing a baby Squid, she was trying to stop it from escaping into it's hole in the rocks, her head was bent low and she was lost in play, when she felt a hard tap on her shoulder. Nattisa looked up and saw Toby, he was looking very agitated and appeared to want her to follow him, so she did exactly that, not knowing where he was taking her at all. He led her to a large group of rocks surrounding a sandy clearing on the sea floor, and there she saw a struggling Dolphin, he was upside down and looked as if he was terrible trouble, in fact he appeared to be drowning!

His tail was lashing the sea floor into a dusty frenzy so bad that Nattisa could hardly see him in all the murky water, he was so frightened and she felt really sorry for him, but, there wasn't much that she could do for him, because she could not approach him till he calmed down a bit, still she came just a bit closer to see if she could see what the problem was, but, not too close in case his lashing tail knocked her flying! All the time Nattisa was approaching him, she was talking to him softly in the language of the Dolphins, it was a language all the Sprites had known, but, seldom had any one spoken it only her, Nattisa spoke softly trying to calm him down, her friend Toby watched all this from a great distance, he had done his bit by bringing her here, now he was keeping well away from the lashing tail, just in case he got hurt.

Suddenly the Dolphin went quiet and still and at first, she thought that it was her voice that had managed to calm him, till she looked closely and realised that he was unconscious and near to death, then Nattisa knew that she must act quickly in order to save him!

She came up to him slowly and carefully, just in case he came round from his faint and started struggling again, she examined him all over for any signs of cuts or wounds that would cause him to act like this, but, she found nothing at all.

Nattisa was looking at him lying helplessly on his back, when she noticed that his mouth was open slightly and protruding from the corner was a white object, on closer inspection Nattisa found the object to be a large piece of white coral and it was very firmly lodged in the back of the Dolphins throat, obstructing his windpipe and causing him to go unconscious and would finally drown him, if it wasn't removed quickly! She then got to work with such urgency and speed, now that she knew what the problem was she could now save him, or try to, for she knew that it was only a matter of some minutes before he would be dead, and she couldn't let that happen:

Nattisa then called to Toby to come to her aid, she found a large length of seaweed and tied one end to the coral in his mouth, after making sure that it was tied securely, she gave the other end to Toby and told him to pull for all that he was worth, the whale did just that and in a few seconds the coral was out, and the Dolphin saved! Nattisa knelt by him and holding him gently, she rocked his head slowly from side to side and got him breathing again, he opened his eyes slowly and looked around him very confused as to where he was, then he focused his eyes on her, hello she said, how are you feeling now, the coral is out and you should be okay in a while, but, how on earth did you come to get it stuck in your throat in the first place, and who are you? He looked at her so confused, he hadn't even got his bearings back yet and she was firing so many questions at him, that he was going dizzy trying to think:

In a croaky voice he said, my name is Macormack, but, who are you, was it you who came and saved me, but, how on earth did you get the coral out it was wedged so tight in my throat, then he realised that he was firing questions at her the same way that she had done to him, so he became quiet, he had to anyway for his throat was very sore, and he was weak from all that struggling and being short of breath.

Nattisa smiled at him, take it easy she said, you must still be feeling very sore and weak, wait till you have recovered a bit more and I shall tell you all that you wish to know, but, for the time being I will introduce us to you, my name is Nattisa and this is Toby my friend, we worked together as a team to get the coral out of your throat, it was wedged so tightly that one alone could not have budged it, so Toby and I did it together, it was a case of my brains and his muscle, and it worked very well!

Macormack looked at them both and they could see that he was grateful to them, he said to them in a weak croaky voice, I don't know how to thank you, I owe you my life, if you had not come along when you did then I would not be here to thank you, I am in debt to you both and I will not forget that in a hurry, one day I shall repay your kindness to me, then still exhausted he settled down to rest for a while.

While Macormack rested, Nattisa told him her story, as I told you before, she said, my name is Nattisa and I am or at least I was a Sprite Princess, my Father was King Danus, and my Mother was Queen Corali they were very great rulers of Coral City, which is where all the Sprites lived, I once had people bowing before me in respect, bringing me presents as I was to be their future ruler, I lived in a very beautiful palace, with so many rooms that you couldn't count them all, I had servants who waited on me hand and foot and did my every bidding, now I am reduced to this, but, strange as it may sound I do not miss the servants waiting on me, or the presents that I used to be given, I miss my parents and my home, and also my people, this I mourn for and nothing else ! They are all gone now, wiped out by a terrible plague, I have never witnessed anyone dying before she told him, it was horrible, she said, the people were dropping all around, it was awful to see their twisted bodies racked with pain, and rotting away, right in front of my eyes, I don't think that I would like to go through that again! Then finally Nattisa told him, how she had helped her parents to pass peacefully out of this world and into the next, and she told him of the prophecy of the Witch, and why she was the only one to be saved from the plague, now if you don't mind, she said to him, I would much prefer to push the terrible happenings to the back of my mind again, and try to get on with the rest of my life the best way that I can!!

When she had finished her tale, Macormack told her sadly, that he had heard all about the plague killing off her people, all the creatures of the sea were warning each other to stay away from the city, in case they caught it too, he said, but, we thought that all the people had perished and no one had escaped, we mourned the loss of your people too, he said, none of the sea creatures knew about you surviving, or we would have helped you, we could have brought you food while you stayed mourning your loss !

Anyway now that the story was told and everything out in the open, they all changed the subject and chatted of other things, the three of them became great friends and Macormack! decided that he would join them in their adventures and go exploring with them. Suddenly Nattisa looked at him, you still haven't told us yet just what you were doing to get that hard lump of coral stuck in your throat, choking you to death!

He looked at her with a silly grin on his face, I am embarrassed to tell you this, he said, but, I was being downright greedy, you see there was this small shoal of fish and I was gulping them down so fast, that I wasn't looking at what I was doing, when one of the crafty fishes went close to that outcrop of rocks, he was trying to avoid being eaten I came down on the fish to snatch it up in my mouth, and as I did this, I sucked inwards and the lump of coral came loose from the rock, it was sucked right back into my throat and there it lodged very firmly, and I couldn't get it out, even though I tried!

That was when I panicked and tried to get it loose, for I knew that if I didn't get it loose then I would die, but , I only succeeded in nearly killing myself, because it was stuck too fast in my throat, and you know the rest, for that is when you found me. I don't know about you two, said Toby, but I am still hungry as I never got a chance to catch any fish for my dinner, which is what I was doing when I discovered you, he said, to Macormack, so it was you who found me, said Macormack to Toby, but, I thought that it was Nattisa who had found me, as it was she who discovered the coral in my throat. No, said Nattisa, it was Toby who found you and he brought me to you, I only found the coral in your throat when you had finally gone quiet, but, as I said before, both myself and Toby worked together as a team to get the coral out, and we succeeded didn't we, so does it really matter who found you, the main thing is that you are safe and well!! You certainly did save me, replied Macormack, and no you are right it doesn't really matter who it was that found me, you make a grand team together, but, tell me, is Toby the new mate that the Witch told you about, are you and he to be the makers of the new race, that the prophecy foretold was coming to Middle Earth;

Oh no, replied Nattisa, Toby is not my future mate, he is my friend and a good one at that, but, that is all he is and nothing else, there will be no new race from my mating with Toby, not that I don't love him, but, not in that way, my love for him is like that of a Sister for a Brother, or a friend for a friend, I do not know who is to be my future mate, I would like to think that he would be similar in looks to me , but, one thing I do know is that it won't be big friendly Toby!

Then I shall help you to find your future mate, said Macormack, the three of us shall search the sea together till we find him for you, then I will know that you are happy and my debt to you will be partly repaid, but, never forgotten.

After all this had been said, they went off in search of a nice tasty meal, as Toby was still complaining that he was absolutely starving, he and Macormack collected some nice tasty tit-bits for Nattisa to eat, then they went off on a rampage eating everything in sight, with Macormack keeping well away from the rocks, especially where the coral was growing, he had learned a valuable lesson, one that he would not forget in a hurry! When they had all eaten their fill, they all settled down for a rest to sleep off their full stomachs, they slept for about an hour, and when all of them had woken up and were fully recovered, the three of them now resumed their searching and exploring, all very determined that they would not rest till the future mate of their friend was found, so that he, whoever he was could begin to create the new race of people as predicted. They were searching for someone who looked like Nattisa in form, but, what they didn't realise was that mates came in many forms, even the most unexpected ones, not even the least bit similar to a beautiful Sea Sprite!!

A few days after they had all met for the first time, they were swimming in a very particularly beautiful part of the sea, the water was a gorgeous azure blue in colour, and it housed the most exotic colourful fishes, bright red and yellow, orange and purple. The coral growing on the rocks were the most perfect in shape and colour, that they had ever seen in all their travels, it was like an heavenly garden, they were examining these exotic fish and corals, when Nattisa spotted the Jellyfish floating on the sea current, it was just floating there bothering no one, so she thought that she would have some fun with the poor creature, Nattisa was always thinking in terms of fun! She swam upwards towards it laughing as she went, and plucking some seaweed from the nearest rocks, she swam to the Jellyfish, once she reached it, she then proceeded to tease and torment the poor creature, tickling it with the seaweed.

She was still teasing the Jellyfish taking care to avoid it's stinging tentacles, when suddenly a dark shadow passed over her head, Nattisa took no notice of it, because she thought that it was Toby, or Macormack swimming over the top of her. She looked to the right of the rocks, because a movement had caught her eye, there she saw Toby and Macormack chasing fish and thoroughly enjoying themselves, she started to smile at their fun, when suddenly the shadow passed overhead again, she stopped smiling and froze in fear, her whole body was shaking and her teeth chattered together! What was it that was shadowing her, she knew that it couldn't be the Whale or the Dolphin, for she could see them over there, so what in heavens name was it!!

The shadow passed again, and the hackles on the back of her neck rose up, and cold shivers ran down her back, Nattisa was really afraid, more of the unknown and what she couldn't see, than what she could see, and she was afraid to look up, but, she had to! So taking all her courage in both hands, Nattisa slowly looked up and looked danger straight in the face, going by overhead was the strangest most curious creature, that she had ever seen before in all of her life.

It was round in shape and had four lumps sticking out of it's body, which on closer inspection turned out to be it's head and legs, the body was completely solid and made from hard shell, she had never seen anything like this creature before!

Nattisa was looking at it, when she was joined by Toby and Macormack, what is this strange looking creature, she asked them, I have never seen it's like before, they both looked at the creature, why it is a Turtle, said Macormack, I have heard all about them from the other sea creatures, and I have seen them swimming in the distance, but, never as close as I am to this one now, isn't it funny looking, quite comical in fact!

No I don't think so, replied Nattisa, I think that he's cute and I suppose to him we must look pretty funny too, now tell me all that you know about them, I want to know everything that there is to know, about our large friend here.

Well for a start, said Macormack, as I told you before, they are called Turtles, and as you can see they have a hard shell cover on their backs and bellies, but, inside of the shell their bodies are soft and fleshy and easy to kill, so they wear these shells for protection!

When the Turtle is attacked it can withdraw the head and legs completely inside the shell, so that the whole of the soft fleshy body is safe from harm.

They are solitary creatures and only meet up when it is time to find a mate, so that they can keep the species going, when the female Turtle is heavy with eggs she swims to the beach, and drags her heavy body out of the water to lay her eggs, why she does not lay the eggs that she is carrying in the sea, no one knows!

For when in the water she is so light and flys through the water hardly making a ripple, her weight does not bother her then, but, once out of water on dry land her body weight doubles with the force of gravity, so she drags this heavy body painfully up the beach, and then digs a large hole in the sand with her flippers.

Once the hole is big enough for her purpose, she then lays hundreds of eggs in that one hole, then covers them with sand to incubate them, when she is satisfied with the job that she has done, she drags herself back down the beach back to the sea, and off she swims, her part in the continuation of her species has been done!

About nine or ten weeks after the laying, hundreds of tiny baby Turtles dig their way out of the sand, and head off towards the direction, that pure instinct tells them is the way to the sea, many of them are picked off by Crabs, many become a tasty meal for the Birds and Sharks, but, that is why she lays so many eggs!!

For out of the hundreds of eggs that she lays, the Mother Turtle knows that only a few will survive, so if she lays enough of them, then at least some will reach the open sea! Once in the sea they head out for the deepest part, and there they seem to disappear for a couple of years, returning only when they are old enough to find a mate for themselves, and to carry on the circle full turn.

That is really all that I have learned about them from other creatures of the sea, that have watched them do these things out of curiosity, if you wish to know more about them than that, then you must ask him, he said, pointing to the Turtle!

Nattisa laughed at that, she played with the Turtle for a while, riding on his back and turning him in the wrong direction, but, he always turned right back again, to think that I was afraid of you, she said softly to the Turtle, why you are so timid and gentle, you wouldn't't' hurt anyone would you!

She stroked him under his head and kissed him, then saying goodbye to him, she let him go, he swam off in his gentle lumbering way, not bothering anyone, he wasn't angry with Nattisa she had been just a pest and now that she had let him go on his way, she was immediately forgotten, Nattisa watched this gentle creature go till he was just a speck in the distance, then she went back to her friends to resume playing, and they had already found something else to interest them, they had forgotten all about the Turtle!

CHAPTER SIX

MILLY

The three of them stayed in this part of the sea for quite a long while, and they loved every minute of their time spent in this beautiful sea garden, the sun shone down on the waters all the time, making the surrounding sea always warm and clear.

They had been there a few weeks now and Toby and Macormack didn't want to leave, there was always plenty of fish and nice things to eat, and plenty of room for them to play in, what more could anyone ask for, they had everything here that they needed, so they did not see any reason to go any further, but, Nattisa did!

She was getting bored here, sure it was beautiful, and true there was always nice things to eat here, but, that did not count for everything, she had nothing to do with her time all day long only play, now that might suit Toby and Macormack, but, not her. I think, she said to them, that we have forgotten the purpose of our mission, and that is to find the mate who is meant for me, the easy living around here has made us soft, and has also made us lazy, sure there is plenty to eat here at the moment, but, the way in which you two eat that won't last long, this place will be barren of food in the next few months or so, hadn't we better leave now then, while there is still plenty of fish and nice things around, and get back to the job in hand, to find my mate so that we can start to create the new race, and fulfil the prophecy!

They looked at Nattisa and then at the beautiful garden, and they had to admit that it was looking a bit the worse for wear, there weren't half as many fish as when they first found it, and the seaweed was nearly all gone, even the coral was looking rather dirty and shabby where they had been playing around it, they had disturbed so much sand from the sea floor with their huge tails, and it had all settled on the coral giving it a very shabby and dirty appearance.

They then knew that Nattisa was right, they were spoiling this beautiful place, and in a bit it would be nothing only a barren desolate place, where nothing could live or grow, and they had not given no thought to that, the future had not concerned them, only the present and the fun that they were having, what an easy life it had been here! Toby and Macormack knew that they had to move on with Nattisa, and let this once thriving place recover itself, and get almost back to normal.

So with one last look around them, they upped stakes and left the garden, heading out for the deeper part of the sea, to see if they could find what they were looking for there, and at least one of them did find what he had been looking for, but, it wasn't a mate for Nattisa that he found, it was one for himself!

The three of them were now swimming in the deepest part of the sea, and Toby who had been here before, warned them to be on the lookout constantly, this is where the larger fish and mammals play, he warned, like the Whales and Sharks, and they play for keeps! I know that the Whales would not hurt you, said Toby, for they are just friendly giants of the sea, but, a Shark now that is a different thing entirely, they will not only hurt you, but, will also kill and eat you, so be on the lookout for danger at all times, for a Shark can stalk you so quietly that despite his size, you will not know that he is behind you until is is too late, and you will be a goner:

They had been travelling in this part of the sea for a few hours now, when they saw a large dark shape coming upon them, they right away thought that it was a Shark, and all of them darted for cover at the same time, but, they darted so fast that they all collided with each other and went tumbling over onto the sea floor, that was when they heard a beautiful tinkling sound, all of them turned round to find out what the sound was, and to their surprise saw a lovely female Whale!

She was beautiful, her size was about the same as Toby or just a bit smaller, she had the most lovely coloured skin, it was pale grey with a pinkish tinge to it, and it was dappled with large dark spots, she was gorgeous!!

Hello, said the female Whale, my name is Milly, but, who are you and what are you doing in this part of the sea, I have not seen you here before, and I know all the creatures who live around here, I'm sure that I would have remembered seeing you before, she said, looking interestedly at Toby, no I don't think that I could forget you, she said, and Nattisa noticed that Toby was looking at Milly in the same way! Nattisa looked at the pair of them making eyes at each other, and she couldn't help smiling at the thought that if Milly had any eyelashes, then she would have been fluttering them at Toby right at this very minute, they were so obviously attracted to each other, and only a blind person could fail to notice that!

She then introduced both them and herself to Milly, my name is Nattisa and this is Toby and Macormack my friends, we are sorry to intrude on your territory, but, we are looking for someone and we are hoping to find him in this area.

Nattisa then told Milly the whole story, she related the tale of her parents and the plague, finally finishing with the Witches prophecy of the new race, and the promised mate that she was supposed to find, well not exactly promised, but, to start a new race then she must have a mate, for she couldn't do it alone!!

Milly looked at her thoughtfully, have you any idea what he will look like, she asked, I may have seen him around the place, "I don't know" replied Nattisa, but, I am hoping that he will look just a bit like me in form.

No, said Milly, I have not seen anyone like you, but, you are welcome to come and stay with me for a while, so that you can have a good look round for this mate of yours, would you like to do that, she asked Nattisa, hopefully, while looking at Toby!

"Yes," replied Nattisa, I think that we would like that very much, " wouldn't we", she said, to Macormack and Toby, Macormack, said yes if you like nodding his head like crazy, he hadn't taken his eyes off Milly since they had first seen her, and he hadn't spoken either, he was dumbstruck by her beauty!

Milly then led the way to her home and they all followed her, especially Toby, he would have followed her anywhere even to the ends of the earth, it was love at first sight!! She led them to a huge outcrop of rock, which was deep in the sea and once up to the rock she started to dive downwards, they followed her blindly not having the least clue as to where she was going, or where they were going either.

Down and down they went, till suddenly out of the gloomy depths, there loomed up right in front of them an enormous cave entrance, Milly swam straight into the cave without any hesitation at all, and she obviously knew where she was going so they just followed! The cave that they entered seemed to go on for miles and was pitch dark, they couldn't see a thing in front of them, and found their way by holding on to each other, although Macormack and Toby had to hold on with their teeth, as they had no hands!

They were getting exhausted and had given up all hope of seeing the light again, when suddenly they broke out of the cave and started swimming upwards at last, up and up they went and again it seemed like miles to the surface, but, eventually they came up and were free of the sea, gasping for breath through the pressure of the deep water!! They were inside a vast Volcano crater that had filled up years ago, the outside rim of the crater was filled with lush green vegetation, it was a paradise even more beautiful than the sea garden, that they had left behind them, Nattisa thought to herself, what a sheltered life she had led, she was nearly eighteen years old, and didn't know that such beautiful places existed in the sea,, what a vast wonderous place I have been living in, without even knowing it!

How on earth did you come to find this place, Nattisa exclaimed, " looking around her in wonder, why, " replied

Milly, I came across it one day when I was being chased by a hungry Shark, which are very numerous in these deep waters.

The Shark had come up on me silently, while I was feeding on Plankton and Krill, it saw me as an easy meal, and was at me before I even knew it was there, she showed them a scar on her flppers where it had bitten her, well anyway, she said, I just panicked and did the only thing that I could to shake off the Shark, I dove downwards!

Deep down I went into the very depths of the sea, but, the Shark wasn't going to be robbed of his meal so easily, he followed me down, on and on we went till I came face to face with the cliff, the Shark had followed me down so far, but, I could tell that he was having trouble with the pressure of the deep water.

He tested himself to the utmost though, he kept on following, till I suddenly came upon the entrance to the cave and shot into it to save myself, I heard the Shark squealing in pain and frustration, both at the water pressure and at losing his meal, but, I didn't stop or look back, I just kept right on going till I finally came out the other side and found all this beauty, she said, looking around her in wonder, this place had been hidden from the eyes of anyone for hundreds of years!

It was and still is an unspoilt paradise, for I have done nothing to disturb the peace and tranquillity of this crater, and she looked at them, I hope that you will treat it in that way too, because, I was so frightened when I first entered the cave, but, when I came out into all this, it sort of calmed me down and quieted my madly beating heart, and I knew that for as long as I live, this will be my home and here I shall be safe! I have been here ever since that day about two years ago I think, there are plenty of fish for me to eat and all the plankton that I need to survive, but, what is more important, the Sharks cannot get at me here as the cave entrance is too deep for them, so here I live, I do venture out into the outside world occasionally for company, but, I always return here for it will always be my safe retreat, and my home!!

Nattisa looked at her, one thing puzzles me, she said, to Milly, you never mentioned what happened to the Shark that followed you," oh didn't I," said Milly, well I found him when I finally got up enough courage to come out of the crater, "he was dead, ". the pressure of the water had bursted his lungs, his gills were shattered wide open and he had drowned, he was half eaten by the fishes when I found him!!

How ironic thought Nattisa, that the creature who had started out wanting to make a meal out of Milly the Whale, had through his own folly, ended up being a meal for someone else, wasn't that the way of the sea world, fish eat fish, and look out for yourself or else, no one else will look out for you, in this world you were on your own. The three of them stayed for a couple of months in the crater with Milly, and she was right, there certainly was plenty of food for them to eat, for as soon as they had nearly exhausted the stock of fish, more would continually come into the crater through the cave entrance, it was a never-ending supply of food.

Toby and Milly spent most of their time together just swimming, or eating, or talking, and it made Nattisa realise when she saw the two of them together, just what she was missing out on, so she and Macormack used to venture out of the crater to search for the would be mate of Nattisa, but, they never found him!

So there came a day when Nattisa knew that she could stay here no longer, for she had to find the one who was intended for her, or the long years would stretch on endlessly and she would die alone, apart from her friends, but, the prophecy would be unfulfilled

So she went to her friends and told them of her intentions to leave, they looked at her in disbelief, to think that she would want to leave this paradise, they just could not understand her at all!

" Why on earth do you wish to leave here", asked Toby?

It has everything that we need, just like the sea garden only with a never-ending food supply, this crater is huge with plenty of room to swim in, we are neither cramped for space or short of food, so why do you want to leave!

"I do not want to leave", said Nattisa, "I have to, it is obvious that I will not find what I am searching for here, I am almost Eighteen years old and the time is right for me to start having babies, so I cannot put it off any longer, I have to go on looking and be true to my destiny, I have no choice at all!!

So they all said their goodbyes and prepared to leave, but, at the last minute Toby could not go through with it, I am sorry Nattisa, he said, I just cannot go with you, I know that I have been with you from the very start, ever since you lost your parents. Through thick and thin we have been together, the good times and the bad I have loved you and stayed with you through them all, but, the time has come to say goodbye to you, I hope that you will find what you are searching for and that you will be happy, " I know that I am," for Milly loves me and I love her too.

We want to stay here forever and have lots of babies, and if we are lucky enough to have a girl, then we shall call her Nattisa after you, said Toby, yes and you are more than welcome to come back and visit us any time that you like, Milly said, too!

I rather thought that you were going to stay behind Toby, Nattisa said, I have known for some time how you felt about each other, your eyes and your actions gave you away, I wish you both well and I would be more than pleased to come back and visit with you, in fact I would have been very offended if you hadn't have invited me back!!

Now we really must be on our way, so they all hugged each other and said their goodbyes all over again, and with tears in everyone's eyes, Nattisa and Macormack left the crater and entered the cave to the outside world, with one last look behind them at Toby and Milly, they went on their way towards the future!

64

When they finally emerged from the cave entrance into the sea outside, Macormack asked Nattisa, " which way shall we go now Nattisa"?

Shall we head back to Coral City, or shall we go on further up North, Nattisa looked at him thoughtfully, " well, she said," I have no wish to return to the city yet, so I think that we shall try further North, I am glad that you are still with me, but, I fear that we shall miss Toby very much, I know replied Macormack, it is a lot safer to travel these waters as a threesome, rather than a twosome anytime, we shall just have to be extra careful that's all and be on the lookout constantly for Danger!!

They started swimming towards the North, and over the next few days they noticed that the water was getting colder and colder all the time, "oh how cold this water is getting" said Nattisa, I think that we made the wrong choice in directions, we shall freeze to death if we dare to go any further, besides which, I don't think that we will find my mate out this way anyway, unless he is an icicle, for I don't think that anything human could possibly survive in these waters, or Animals either, she thought :

Suddenly Nattisa found out just how wrong she could be, as she and Macormack were nearly knocked flying by a large herd of fast swimming animals, they were grey in colour and had a chubby body ending with flippers, a nicely shaped head with whiskers and two large cheeky eyes, they also had flippers on the side of their body too.

"What on earth are these animals," she said to Macormack, he looked at them carefully and with much thought, I am not sure, he said, but, I think that they are called Seals, I have never seen them before, nor do I know anything about them, except what I have heard from the other sea creatures who have had close encounters with them, but, I can guess from the description that I was given, that these are the creatures mentioned.

"Why, said Nattisa the wonders of this sea that I have lived in for nearly Eighteen years now, will it never cease to amaze me, I do not think that I have been living up till now, just merely existing and missing out on all this, as she said this, she turned and looked around her, with wonder in her eyes, then in the distance she spotted something else although what it was she couldn't say yet, they were too far away! By the Gods in the Heavens, she said, what are those creatures swimming in the distance, " why I do believe that they are Sea Sprites dressed in black and white garments, I wonder could one of these be the mate that I am looking for"!!

Nattisa took off at great speed despite the cold water slowing her down, Macormack followed her as fast as he could, but, he too was feeling the coldness of the water, however at the speed that he could swim, he was soon in front of her. When they finally came abreast of the creatures they soon discovered that they weren't Sea Sprites after all, but, some kind of underwater bird with a black jacket on their backs, and a white shirt on their fronts, and these birds were swimming in complete and utter harmony with the Seals!

Nattisa was amazed that two such different creatures could swim so placidly together, without trying to harm each other, then she thought to herself, why Macormack and I are different creatures aren't we, and we swim in harmony without trying to hurt each other, so why not them, she thought, as she looked at the strange wonderous creatures. " What are they"? She asked Macormack, as she pointed at the new creatures, but, he was as mystified as she was, this time I do not know what they are, I have never seen or heard of their like before, he said!!

They were both poised motionless in the sea looking at the strange animals, and they were both very puzzled by what they saw, suddenly they were joined by another strange, but, familiar creature, he was the same size as Macormack, only different in shape and colour and his nose and fins were not the same either, and yet they were similar!

Hello, said the creature, you two, look rather lost, is there any way that I can be of help to you?

Nattisa and Macormack looked at him, "who are you"? Nattisa asked the creature. And why do you look so much like my friend Macormack here, " I look like your friend because I am a Porpoise, a distant relative to the Dolphin, so although we are not exactly the same in looks, we are still very similar, enough to be mistaken for each other from a great distance, we are what you would call distant cousins!

Now that we have got all that sorted out, said the Porpoise, in what way can I be of assistance to you, for you appear to be in some difficulty and I will help in any way that I can, so please tell me what your problem is!

We have no great problem really, said Nattisa, we were just wondering what those animals over there were called, and saying this, she pointed at the swimming Birds.

The Porpoise followed her pointing finger and looked at the creatures that she was pointing at, those are called Penguins, he said, I thought everyone around here knew the Penguins, they are such friendly creatures that you can't help, but, know them! But, I am not from around here, said Nattisa, I am a stranger to these parts and I have seen many animals around here that I don't know the names of, I am or was a Princess in the part of the sea from where I came, and I have led a very sheltered life, in fact I am only just starting to learn about things and animals that I never knew before, and this makes me more than just a bit angry, to think that I have never seen the likes of any of these strange and wonderful sights before!!

Then come along with me, said the Porpoise, I will take you further up North and show you some really beautiful sights, they will take your breath away with their beauty! I will show you the Icebergs made entirely from Snow and Ice, they are so sheer and glassy, that when the Sun shines down on them they sparkle and shimmer and the Sun's rays flash off them like so many precious Jewels in the sea.

And I will also show you the Northern Lights, they are a spectacular display of coloured lights, they flash and crackle in the sky, in a myriad of many bright colours and they also reflect off the snow-covered ground, no one knows what causes this phenomenon to take place, but, it is a marvellous sight to see, so please will you come with me? I am sorry, replied Nattisa, but, I have already been here too long, for as much as I would love to see all these breath-taking sights, I am afraid that I can't go with you, for I am already having my breath taken, not by your wonderous sights, but, by the coldness of your part of the sea, which I am not used to!

My skin is blue with the icy cold and my teeth are chattering hard enough to break, I am sorry, but, we must leave your part of the sea for warmer waters as soon as we can, or I fear that we shall freeze to Death!!

I did not know that, said the Porpoise, I thought that you were like me when I saw you swimming in these waters, I thought that the cold waters did not bother you either, but, come we are wasting time talking, come let us hurry and get you back to warmer waters as soon as we possibly can, before any harm befalls you:

And saying this, he bobbed down so that Nattisa could climb onto his back, hop on board, he said, I will get you back to warmer waters quicker and safer than you trying to swim there, for if you are already turning blue, then it won't be long before your whole body seizes up and you die from the cold, come we have not a moment to loose!!

So Nattisa climbed onto his back as best as she could, and he in turn swam for all that he was worth back towards the South and the warmer climate, and he was followed in close pursuit by a very cold Dolphin with a blue iced up nose!

At the rate that the Porpoise swam it took only a few hours to reach the Southern part of the sea, and Nattisa and Macormack noticed that the water was getting warmer all the time, she was losing her blue skin and felt much better.

She was also getting some feeling back into her fingers and toes, and her teeth had stopped chattering and when she looked back at Macormack, she noticed that he was no longer dragging behind, but, was swimming a lot faster and his nose was no longer blue! By the time the Porpoise had finally stopped to let Nattisa off his back, she was feeling a lot better, the water was now lovely and warm and in fact she felt GREAT!!

"Oh, Mr Porpoise, how can I possibly thank you for all that you have done for us," you have been so kind and you have really saved our lives you know, if it wasn't for your strength and great speed we would never have got back alive, we shall never forget this act of kindness and if ever you should need help at any time in the future, please do not hesitate to contact us in some way, we shall never refuse you a favour of any kind, it would help to repay you in part for your kindness, as we owe you so very much! Thank you for the offer of help in the future, he said, but, my name is not Mr Porpoise a" Porpoise is what I am," my name is Theo, and one day I may take you up on your offer of repayment in the form of help, one day in the future you may just hear from me!

Now I really must be on my way, he said, although I can live quite comfortably in both climates of water, just by the taking on or shedding of extra blubber, I much prefer the colder climate, though if you asked me why, "I don't think that I could tell you why," I just much prefer to be at a cold temperature than a warm, perhaps I'm bonkers!

So once again Nattisa and Macormack were saying goodbye to a creature who had befriended them, and who they liked very much and they were sorry to see him go, both of them poised motionless and watched him swimming off into the distance till he had completely vanished from sight, then they resumed their journey and this time it was towards the South!

Well where to now, said Macormack, as they swam side by side, shall we go back to the crater and spend some time with Toby and Milly, or shall we pass them by and leave them in peace for a while longer, we could always go back to the sea garden and rest up for a while there!

"Yes that would be a good idea," said Nattisa, even though I would love to see both our friends again, it is only six weeks since last we saw them, I know that they told us to come back and visit them, but, I think that they would both agree, that six weeks is not a long enough time to come visiting so soon...

So I think that we shall by pass them for a while longer, and go on to the sea garden to rest up as you have suggested, and this is what they did do, they swam past the crater where their friends Toby and Milly had made their home into a love nest, and kept heading on towards the South and the sea garden!

It took them about three weeks of swimming before they were anywhere near their goal, and that was with rests in between to feed and sleep, but, they were really looking forward to reaching the garden and spending some time there feeding up properly, also to getting plenty of well-earned rest, before deciding where to go from there.

Nattisa saw the group of rocks which were the boundary around the sea garden," Oh look," Macormack, she cried, just another hundred yards or so and we'll be there, I can almost taste. those delicious exotic fish right now," oh come on let's hurry, she said, I can't wait to get there, so let us put all speed on now!

They swam as fast as they could and finally arrived at the rock boundary around the garden, Macormack was the fastest so he got there first and he wished that he hadn't, he took one look over the rocks and stopped dead in his tracks with his mouth wide open in shock, Nattisa took one look at his face, and with fear in her heart, she said, "what on earth is the matter my friend, you have gone as white as a wave crest, and why are you so shocked"!

She came up beside him and she too stopped dead and looked in horror and disbelief at the ghastly sight that met with her eyes, as she looked into the once beautiful garden! The exotic oasis: was no more, everything that was beautiful about it had been completely wiped out, there was not one piece of colourful coral left, not one exotic fish or bright green seaweed, all that they saw as far as the eye could see, were hundreds of brown rolling balls with sharp long needles or thorns sticking out from them, they had devoured everything in sight, the whole of the garden had been utterly destroyed by this horrid ravenous creature called the Crown of Thorns Starfish, a creature that will and does eat anything and everything that it can get it's teeth into!

On seeing what had become of her sea garden Nattisa couldn't take anymore, she just sat right down where she was on the sea floor and cried her eyes out, "oh Macormack," she said, "what on earth are we going to do now and where shall we go"?

"I do not know," replied Macormack, I am tired and weary and I have had enough of trailing around the sea looking for this non-existent mate of yours!"

On hearing this statement from the only friend who had stayed with her through thick and thin, Nattisa cried even harder, she felt really sad and betrayed by his words! " I am sorry Nattisa," Macormack said, I did not mean to hurt or offend you by my harsh words, "it is just the tiredness speaking for me," please take no notice of what I say. Nattisa looked at him with tears in her eyes, "no you are right," she said, I too have had enough searching for a while, I think that now would be a good time to go back and visit our friends in the crater, it will be three weeks or so, before we can get back to them, making twelve weeks in all, just a long enough time to return for a visit.

"Yes I really think that would be the best choice, to return to the crater and rest and have some fun again with our own dear friends, with plenty of good things to eat and nothing to do all day long, it won't take long to get back to our old selves again! And without waiting to say or think anymore, they immediately rose up, and with no more ado, they started on the long journey, back North, to the crater and their friends!! The way that they were travelling was a long and weary one, with no where along the way to rest properly, and no shelter to hide from any danger that should befall them! But, still the two friends journeyed on together for they knew that they had to reach the crater, it was their only salvation in this savage part of the sea, they must have good food and plenty of rest to recover some of their energy and strength back, before they collapsed from sheer exhaustion!

Macormack went off frequently to get food for them both, always leaving Nattisa behind resting, usually hidden away in some obscure niche in the rocks supposedly safe from danger of any kind, or so he thought, for it was while he was on one of these food hunts, that Nattisa did a foolish thing that nearly cost her life!! She had been resting in the rocks for what seemed like ages to her, Macormack had been gone for some time now, he was gorging himself on fish and thinking that she was safe and sound, but, "little did he know just how wrong he was"...

Nattisa was starving and when she saw a large shoal of fish go by, she decided that she couldn't wait for Macormack to return, so she left the safety of the rocks and went off to catch her own food, the fish looked so inviting and she was so Hungry!

So without giving it a second thought, she darted straight up out of her hiding place and headed right for the shoal of delicious looking fish, and her mouth was drooling. Nattisa found that even though she was right in the middle of the shoal of fish, she was having great difficulty in catching them, for one thing she was so weak and tired from her long searching, and they were darting here there and everywhere in fear.

Nattisa could both feel and smell their fear, but, she was so hungry that she didn't stop to think what they were frightened of, she thought that it was herself that was making them so afraid, but, she was wrong, so very, very wrong, and once again she had put herself into real life or death Danger!!

Suddenly Nattisa caught one of the fish, and being so hungry she bit it's head clean off from the rest of the body, after that it was easy, she grabbed fish by the handful taking a bite here and a bite there, she was in her element, the pieces of fish were just slipping down her throat and she was taking a second bite, before she had even had time to chew the first bite, that's how hungry she had become, and greedy!!

However it was the struggling fish that she had bitten and left for dead that was causing the trouble, for they were attracting the Sharks that had been stalking the fish all along, in fact it had been the Sharks who had caused the fish to be afraid in the first place, their fear had only been partly because of Nattisa, but, mostly it had been the Sharks the greatest enemy of all the sea creatures, including Nattisa! The Sharks were moving ever closer to their prey all the time and the fish sensed this, but, Nattisa didn't, she was so hungry that she saw only the fish and was blind to everything else, at this moment only the needs of her body were important nothing else. Suddenly some sort of sixth sense warned her that danger was near, maybe it was because her stomach was getting fuller and she was feeling a bit better, so therefore she wasn't quite as preoccupied with food as she had been earlier on.

Whatever the reason was, Nattisa knew that danger was very near to her at this moment, because the hackles at the back of her neck had risen in fear, and horrible shivers ran down her back giving her goose bumps!

Nattisa stopped eating and very slowly turned around, she didn't turn fast for fear of attracting attention to herself, but she needn't have worried how fast or slow to turn round, because the Sharks had seen her anyway, they were watching very closely both her and the fish, healthy and wounded through Nattisa, they were all in danger now from these dreadful vicious carnivores of the sea!!

The silly careless Sprite was overcome with fright and she couldn't move a muscle, " oh what a fool I have been," she said to herself, " why on earth did I not stay in my hiding place, where Macormack had left me, and where I would have remained safe," " why did I let my hunger and greed get the better of me," and she thought back to her own words, when Milly had told them of the Shark who had tried to eat her, and had ended up through his own foolishness being eaten himself .

What was it I said to them, thought Nattisa," oh now I remember," I said, Fish eat Fish in this sea world and look out for yourself or else, it went something like that anyway! Suddenly one of the Sharks who was on the outer edge of the fish shoal got tired of waiting, he moved quickly forward towards the shoal of which Nattisa was right in the centre, she was so afraid that she urinated in the water, it was the worst thing that she could have possibly done, for the Sharks smelt the fear in her urine and this smell of fear exited them into attacking!

The smell of fear in the water drove them crazy and they dived into the shoal of fish and began a frenzied feeding spree, the crazy Sharks were tearing the fishes to pieces, and it was at that moment in time that Nattisa high tailed it and fled for her life!

She swam at the fastest speed that her still exhausted body could manage, and never turned around once to look behind her, but, she knew without having to look that they were still following her, she was quarry to them and she was afraid, the Sharks sensed this and they weren't about to let her get away so easily, Nattisa was going to make a grand meal for them all, if there was enough of her to go around, she was too thin!

Nattisa swam as hard as she could, but her speed was slowing down a great deal, what with the sea current being against her and still being very tired, she knew that her pace of speed was slowing down and the Sharks were catching her up, soon she would be too exhausted to go any further, and that would be it, the end of her journey was near!! The sea current was really pushing quite strongly against her now, it made her every movement sheer agony, every nerve, muscle and sinew in her body was stiff and racked with pain, but, she just had to keep going till she found a place where she could take refuge from these hungry beasts, Nattisa was just thinking this when in the distance she saw three more large grey shapes heading towards her," oh no," she thought, here comes more of the rotten things, I am doomed, they are all around me and I have no chance at all to get away from them, " I might as well give up," she cried aloud !

"What sort of defeatist talk is that, coming from a so called Princess", said one of the grey shapes coming towards her fast, I leave you hidden in the rocks while I go off to search for food for us, and see the mess that you go and get yourself into, and me thinking that you were safely hidden away!

"Oh Macormack," Nattisa said, as she recognised his voice, you have come back and found me, just in the nick of time too, I might add, but, who is that with you? " I thought that you were all more Sharks coming to gobble me up for dinner"!!

" Why I have brought Toby and Milly to see you, said Macormack, they were out of the crater having a nosey at the outside world, and I met them, back together to get you, but, let us discuss all this later when we have more time, for at the moment I fear that we have more pressing matters that must come first! On saying this he and Toby shot past her and started to attack the Sharks, while Milly took Nattisa under her wing or flipper, and swore to protect the Sprite and let no harm befall her, not while she was alive at least.

So both of them moved back into the slight shelter of the steep sea cliff, hardly any cover at all, but, better than nothing, and once installed there they proceeded to watch the terrible fight, that was taking place between a Killer Whale, a Dolphin and a group of ferocious hungry Sharks, but, there was no doubt who was going to win, it was a no contest situation right from the start of round one!!

The Sharks came in slowly and stealthily for the kill, but, they had no chance, they were much too slow and had no way of avoiding the much lighter and faster Dolphin, and the Whale who didn't need speed, as he had weight on his side, but, even so he was very much faster than the Sharks, who were no match for him at all!

Macormack came up over and over, tupping the Sharks quite hard in their gills with his long solid nose, he bursted their gills which allowed water to enter into their lungs thus drowning them, he did this to each one that he encountered.

Soon the sea floor was strewn with the bodies of either dead or dying Sharks, and what escaped Macormack, were in turn killed by Toby the Whale, he wasn't as quick as the Dolphin, and he couldn't come up underneath them to tup their gills and drown them, But, he was not to be out done by the Dolphin, he had weight and great strength on his side and he just came straight on at them, hitting them smack bang in the middle of their foreheads, and completely crushing their skulls, killing them instantly!

Nattisa and Milly watched this dreadful battle from the safety of their hiding place, and they were not going to come out till all this was over!

The sea looked terrible from what had taken place in it, there were great cloudy sand storms brought up from the sea floor, caused by the force of the battle that had taken place, and mingled in the clouds of sand was the deep red blood of the dead or dying Sharks, the scene before their eyes was horrible enough to give them nightmares.

The sea bed everywhere they looked , was covered in blood and guts, large strips of flesh and fallen Sharks, that had become a meal for the fish that they had hunted only hours before, the bodies were being devoured before they even reached the sea floor, Nattisa looked around her in horror, I need to get away from here as quickly as possible, she said to Milly, I have to reach the safety of the crater in order to rest and get back some of my sanity, before it's too late, then she leaned over and brought all the contents of her stomach up onto the sea bed, and watched in disgust as the wretched fishes came darting over and began to eat even that!!

What a revolting sight, said Nattisa, as she looked at the disgusting fish enjoying their foul-smelling feast, then she turned to her friends," come my friends, let us make all haste to get away from this gruesome battlefield, for if I do not get some peace, quiet and rest in the heavenly crater, then I fear that I shall go insane. The three large friends looked at her face and saw that she was deadly serious, her face was a sickly shade of yellow, and she was swaying with complete exhaustion!

Suddenly as they were looking at her, Nattisa gave way at the knees and collapsed, she was out cold and her friends knew that they had to get her out from here pretty quickly, for she was really out for the count and they feared for her life!!

CHAPTER SEVEN

THE SEARCH ENDS HERE

Macormack, Toby and Milly, had to work fast, and between them they managed to nudge her gently with their noses onto Toby's back, after which they travelled at top speed back towards the crater, through the Shark infested waters, to safety!

At the speed that they were swimming it only took them a short while to reach their destination, the greatest difficulty that they encountered on the journey was when diving down to the cave entrance, Nattisa kept sliding down towards Toby's head and more than just a few times, she nearly fell off!

Then there was getting her through the long tunnel to the crater, the tunnel was not very wide and with Nattisa's legs hanging over Toby's side, they were sticking out too much, and kept catching the side of the tunnel walls.

By the time that they finally got her out into the basin on the other side of the cave entrance, she was in a bad way, her face was now grey in colour and her arms and legs were cut and scratched very badly, as the three friends took her over to the beach and laid her gently down on the sand, they knew that it would take a long time with plenty of rest and good food, plus lots of looking after, before she would be back to her normal fun-loving self!!

And time is exactly what it did take, a whole six long months went by before Nattisa was anywhere near her former self, and for at least three of those six months she was so ill, and so much in shock that they thought that she was going to die! Macormack stayed by her side morning, noon and night, he saw to her every need, bringing her food and drink and staying with her constantly while she slept.

The only time he left her was when he was so exhausted through lack of sleep, that Toby and Milly insisted that he should get some rest, but, even then he wouldn't leave till they promised to watch over her carefully, and to call him right away if she should wake up and ask for him, though she never did, she still slept soundly without him by her side, in fact, for months, she never knew whether he was there or not! " Why do you guard her so carefully"? Asked Toby!

You know that no harm can come to her while she rests here in the crater guarded by us, Macormack looked at his friend and his answer to the question was simply said, " I guard Nattisa so carefully, because I love her," replied Macormack;

Toby looked at him, and replied, I love Nattisa too, and so does Milly, we can see to her needs just as well as you do, so that you can get some much needed rest! I know that you and Milly love Nattisa too, said Macormack, but, you love her like a brother for a sister, while I love her like a sweetheart, just as you and Milly love each other and want to have babies, that is the way that I love Nattisa!!

Toby was dumbstruck with shock, "how can you love her in that way," he said to Macormack "why you are a Dolphin and she is a Sea Sprite," there is so much difference in the way that you both look, I don't understand how you can say to me, that you feel the same for Nattisa as I feel for Milly, it would be impossible, wouldn't it "!

"I don't know, replied Macormack, I do not understand it myself, all I know is that since way back I have never been interested in the females of my kind, I always thought that there was something wrong with me, till I met Nattisa, why the very first time I laid eyes on her, I knew there was something special about her, and that there could be something special between us two, in fact I saw from the very first that she was meant for me, and I was meant for her, I know that sounds stupid, but, it's true !

When our eyes first met my heart skipped a beat, and when she told me the story of her past and the prophecy of the new race, I thought that you were to be her promised mate, I was so jealous of you and filled with hatred, that I wanted to kill you, and literally tear your body to pieces with my teeth.

"Why I can't believe that of you," replied Toby, your race is so kind and gentle, I have never known a Dolphin yet who would intentionally want to hurt another creature of the sea, except for Sharks!

Well you have known one now, said Macormack, for my words are true, I was so relieved when Nattisa told me that you were not her future mate, and I was even more relieved when you and Milly met and fell in love, because that meant that I could have Nattisa all to myself, I can't tell you how happy I was at the thought of all those wonderful long months alone with my love, but, look where it's got me!

I had to leave her alone for long periods while I hunted for food for us, I was afraid to leave her behind and too afraid to take her with me, out in the open sea with no shelter from danger, so I left her safely hidden or so I thought my actions have nearly robbed me of the one that I love!!

Toby looked at him sadly, but, what sort of future do you possibly think could be in store for you both, even if Nattisa did return your love what could you do about it? " I mean you are so different in shape and form, how will you manage," I don't know, replied Macormack, but, one thing I do know is that it was meant to be, for Nattisa and I are to be the creators of the New Race!!

"How can you talk in that way, said Toby, your words are nothing but blasphemy, and it's only sheer luck that the Gods don't strike you down for speaking them. And with that parting shot he swam away angrily, muttering under his breath as he went, stupid Dolphin, he said to himself, just who does he think that he is, to talk in that way, why his words are just nonsense that's all!

"Where did he get the stupid idea that he and Nattisa are to create the new race, Nattisa will, that's true, when she finds her promised mate that is when the new race will be created, but, not with Macormack, that would be impossible!

"No, thought Toby, our friend the Dolphin is definitely getting idea's above his station, and with that, Toby went off to find Milly, to tell her, what the stupid Dolphin had said, and to catch some fish as he was feeling a bit hungry.

Macormack sadly watched as his angry friend swam off into the distance, " I wonder why Toby got so angry when I told him of my feelings for Nattisa, I mean, I know that she and I are not the same shape, or form, but, what would be so strange or unusual about us being meant for each other, as I think we are meant to be together as mates!

Take Toby and Milly for example, they are both similar in shape and form, they are both Whales, but, not from the same race, he is a Black and White, Killer Whale, while she is a Grey Whale, still they love each other and have already mated to try to have little ones, Toby didn't think that the difference between him and Milly mattered, "so why should it bother him so much about the difference between Nattisa and himself," Macormack just didn't understand his friend at all!!

And looking once again into the distance after Toby, he swam off back to his duties, back to Nattisa, so that he could make her well again and tell her of his feelings! As the days went by, the anger of Toby's words faded and the two of them got back on more friendly terms, the worry that they both felt for Nattisa replaced any anger that had passed between them, and brought them closer together again.

For both Macormack and Toby, and also Milly, were really worried about the fate of their dear friend, she was showing no signs of recovery yet and still slept the sleep of near death, but, they needn't have worried quite so much, for it was not illness that caused this deep sleep, it was plain exhaustion from weeks of hardly any proper food, and through the constant danger around them very little sleep either.

Nattisa remained in this state of deep sleep for at least for three months, then she slowly began to recover with the help of her friends, who stayed by her side through those long months, looking after her very need and seeing to her every comfort.

And they also stayed by her side for the next three months while she was convalescent, so in all it took a whole six months from Nattisa first collapsing to her complete recovery, thanks to her friends, especially Macormack:

As she slowly got her strength and energy back, Nattisa and Macormack went swimming together and the stronger she got, then the further they went, spending more and more time alone together, as Toby and Milly were too caught up with their own lives, for Milly was expecting a baby any day now and she and Toby were delighted! Macormack and Nattisa became closer together with each day that passed, they swam together and laughed a lot, and played games of tag and chase, he brought her presents of Oysters and Sea Anemones to put in her hair.

He also brought her lovely Mother of Pearl and Coral combs, plus real Pearls from the Oysters to make into necklaces to adorn her neck, Macormack was in fact courting Nattisa, as any other male of her race would have courted her in the past! They were sitting on the rocks one day, in the middle of the Lagoon in the crater, he was tickling her with his fins, when they suddenly heard Milly scream out in pain and saw Toby racing towards them at top speed.

Nattisa, Macormack, he cried, please come quickly, Milly is about to give birth and she is crying out in such pain, I am sure that something is going to go wrong, please come with me right away, my Milly is in much pain and I don't know how to help her! Don't worry, said Nattisa, she will be okay, this is your first child and you do not know it, but, all females go through this sort of pain when they are in the labour of childbirth, it will not do Milly any good if she sees the state of panic that you are in, so please try to calm down before we return to her.

Toby led the way back quickly to where he had left Milly having her baby, and he tried his best to stay calm and not show his fear to her, but, it was really hard and he was shaking with dread of what was happening to the female that he loved!

Milly was in such constant pain and even Nattisa began to get worried, she knew that there should be some pain in childbirth, she had learned that much by being present at other births, but, not this much and she too began to fear that something was wrong!

The poor Whale was writhing first one way and then the other, crying out in pain all the time, that's when Nattisa realised that Milly's baby was stuck in it's Mother's birth canal, she knew that she would have to act fast, or both of them would be lost! So she quickly approached the writhing female and acting on instinct alone, she pushed her hand and arm into the Whale's abdomen, and once in there Nattisa grabbed hold as hard as she could of the baby Whale and pulled for all that she was worth!!

Suddenly she felt a huge pressure pushing her arm out and she drew back quickly, all at once there was a loud whooshing noise and out into the water shot the baby Whale, it was covered in a cloud of blood and along with it came the afterbirth still attached!

Nattisa went to work right away on the baby, while Toby and Macormack looked after Milly, who was crying out for her child, Nattisa bent over the new born calf and cut the birth cord, then she started to clean it up, that was when she noticed that it wasn't moving, the bereft Sprite did everything that she knew how to make the calf move, but, it never would for it was dead!!

Nattisa dropped to her knees on the sandy bottom of the Lagoon and putting her head into her hands, she wept like she did the time when her parents died and when Blip her friend the Dolphin, was taken from her, " oh no," she wept, how can I tell them! " How can I tell Toby and Milly that the child they had been waiting for so long, had arrived in this world stillborn, never to open it's eyes and see their faces, or hear their voices, never to feel their touch, or swim in the sea with them, this poor child would never be able to do any of those things ever, not ever at all!!

Suddenly, she heard another cry of pain from Milly, Nattisa turned around quickly, Milly shouldn't still be in pain, she thought, "had the poor Whale seen her dead child," was that why she was crying out in pain, but, no, when Nattisa reached the side of her friends, she was just in time to see another calf being born, "Twins," Nattisa thought, Milly had been carrying Twins all along!

No wonder the poor Whale was in so much pain, the dead baby had been lodged sidewards inside of her, while the live baby was desperately trying to get out into the world outside, the cruel world of the sea and it had made it with the help of Nattisa, she looked at her happy friends who did not know yet about the dead baby, she thought to herself, now they will have a child to see, touch and feel them, and what a pity that they couldn't have had them both!

As Nattisa wept, she could hear Toby in the background he was so happy, he said to Milly," oh Milly what a clever Lady you are, we wait all this time for one baby and you go and produce two," "Twins, he said, and looked in awe at his mate, I love you very much Milly, said Toby, and I am very proud of you.

Milly looked back at him, thankyou Toby, she said, but, it takes two to make babies you know, so I could not have done it without you and I certainly couldn't have delivered them safely without Nattisa there to help, at that she looked around her, speaking of Nattisa, she said, where has our dear friend got to!

I have not seen her since the birth of our first child, Toby looked around too, " why she is over there, he said, "see, she is kneeling by the big boulder, over there on the sand seeing to our child, and saying this Toby called over to Nattisa. Hi there Nattisa, how is our child doing, " this one is a Boy, he said, looking down proudly at his son, " what sex is the one that you have over there, he asked?

Nattisa looked at him sadly," it was a Girl," she answered, Toby got really exited then, he didn't hear the word was, or see the sadness in her eyes, she was too far away for him to see that, but, he heard the word Girl and that was enough for him, he turned back to his mate Milly then, and his new son, bubbling with great joy!

Imagine that, he said, to Milly, we have one of each, a Boy and a Girl, our Family is complete we won't need to have any more children if you don't want to, Toby said, remembering how much pain she had been in just a short while ago, but, as Milly looked down at the new born calf at her side, she had already forgotten all that, the fear and the pain were all in the past now, replaced by happiness at her new Family! However if Toby had not seen the tears in her eyes or heard the past tense was, when Nattisa talked of the new born calf, someone else had seen and heard these things, Macormack had taken notice of her words and her pain, and leaving the side of his happy friends, he came over to enquire what was troubling her.

On approaching her side, he asked, "what is the matter Nattisa, why are you so sad?"

Then he followed her gaze down to the dead calf lying motionless on the sea floor, " oh no," said Macormack, " is the poor thing dead," how and why did she die, did she hit her head on the rocks as she was being born, for she did shoot out from her Mother with such force at the birth, so maybe that's what happened, or was she dead before then, what do you think happened Nattisa, he asked?

Nattisa did not answer his question, her head was down and her shoulders were shaking with the sobbing of many tears, Macormack looked across at his friends doting on their other new born, who by this time was swimming around exploring, " how are we going to tell them, he said, and he too had tears in his eyes!

Suddenly they saw Toby coming towards them, he was coming to look at his little Girl and he was wondering why she wasn't up and about by now, swimming around like her energetic Twin Brother was doing.

As he approached them he noticed their sad faces and his heart dropped like a stone quivering with fear, " why are your faces so sad, he asked?

Surely this is a time for happiness, there can be no room for sadness on a day like this, he dropped his eyes down to look at his new born Girl child lying so still on the sea floor, his eyes rested on her motionless body and the words froze on his tongue! " Why does my precious child not move, he said, she is so still that you would swear that she was dead, but, it couldn't be, could it, she is not dead is she, please tell me that she is only sleeping, still tired from the trauma of her birth, please tell me that is so, she can't be dead and his voice convulsed into deep sobs of pain!!

"Why did this have to happen, he sobbed to his friends, we were so happy, why did she have to die and how will I break the sad news to Milly, I don't know Toby, replied Nattisa, perhaps it wasn't her time to be born yet and she was trying to come into this world too soon, or maybe it was because you were too proud and happy, I don't think that it was meant for anyone to be too happy or proud in this life, do you, for if you are then the sea Gods always punish you in some way!

Maybe they took your child back to live with them to punish you for your pride, only the Gods themselves know the answer and I don't think that they are going to tell us what reason they had for taking your child, one thing that you can be sure of though, whatever reason they had, your child is in good hands now, I can bet you that my Mother and Father will be looking after her, she will be happy with them I know that for a fact, for they took good care of me didn't they!!

Toby nodded his head in answer as he was too choked with tears to talk, then he sadly swam back to his mate, somehow he had to break the news to her though heaven knows how she was going to take it, or how he was going to tell her, gently was the way, but, he knew that no matter how gentle he was, Milly would still take the news badly! Nattisa and Macormack sadly watched as Toby went back to Milly with his heart broken, Nattisa said, Macormack my dear friend I think that it's time we left our friends alone for a while, both to get used to their new Son and to get over their grief for the dead child, besides I think that I would like to return to the city where I was born and spent my childhood years growing up, for I have the feeling that I am soon to meet my new mate, but, we must take care of one last duty before we leave here. Macormack looked down at the tiny still calf on the sea floor, you mean to bury the little one, he said, " yes, said Nattisa, Toby and Milly are too upset to do it and she looked across at their weeping friends lost in grief, with a confused new born calf swimming around them wondering why his parents were so sad!

We must do it, said Nattisa, they are in no fit state to even think of burying their calf, we cannot leave the poor thing out here in the open to rot or be eaten by the fishes, there is no one else to perform the task, so we will wait till nightfall and bury the little one when everyone else is asleep.

And that is what they did, when night fell and they were sure that everyone was fast asleep although rather a fitful sleep for Toby and Milly, but, sleep all the same, Nattisa collected together all the long lengths of sea weed that she could find and tied them together, then she and Macormack found a good spot and began to dig there a fairly large hole in the sand on the sea floor.

Taking one end of the seaweed rope she tied it firmly around the tail of the calf, then she and Macormack grabbed hold of the other end and holding tight and firm, they began to drag the body slowly towards the grave which was to be it's last resting place, they then buried the lot including the seaweed and once that was done they swept. the sand clean and it was as if the poor child had never been.

When the heart breaking task was completed, Nattisa and Macormack then left a message written in the sand for their friends to read when they awoke from their sleep, and taking one last look around them at their sleeping friends and the crater which had been their home for so long now, they then sadly made their way towards the cave entrance to the outside world and back to Coral City, only one pair of eyes saw them leaving that day, the eyes of the young calf, who was too young to ever tell anyone what he had seen for he was too young to talk yet, he wasn't even concerned about their leaving either, because he didn't know or understand who they were, he just flicked his tail happily and swam off to chase the fish.

On emerging from the cave entrance into the open sea, the friends then headed off to the South towards the sea garden, and further on after that Coral City which was their goal. I wonder if the sea garden has recovered yet from the damage caused by the Crown of Thorns Starfish, said Macormack, to Nattisa!

"I don't know, replied Nattisa, it may have done, it is quite a while since we were last there, anyway we shall soon see for ourselves if the garden has recovered, for if we travel at a good speed it won't take us more than a few weeks to reach it. " I mean, we are not as weak and ailing as we were the last time that we visited the place, so we should make good going even allowing stops for frequent rests to eat and sleep, we should be there in about sixteen days at the most.

They had been heading South for about two days, when they found an ideal place to rest and have a good meal, they needed to replace some of the energy that they had used up in swimming for a great distance between stops, the place was a fairly large clearing on the sea bed with plenty of vegetation and lots of varied sea life.

Around the edge of the clearing was a formation of rocks providing cover from danger, in the centre of the formation of rocks there was a huge cave which they both agreed would make an excellent sleeping place in which to spend the night.

Macormack said to Nattisa, how would it be if I went out to round up some food for us, while you stay here and collect plenty of fresh green weeds to make a comfortable bed on which to spend the night in safety and comfort.

Yes, said Nattisa, that would be a splendid idea, let us waste no time in putting your idea into action for I am feeling a bit tired and hungry, so without wasting any more time they put all their energy into the task of preparing for nightfall!

However, before Macormack left to hunt for food, he decided that he would check the cave out first, just to make sure that it was safe for Nattisa to enter, so leaving her outside in the clearing he slowly entered into the darkness of the unknown cave! Once inside he was able to have a good look around, the cave was huge and very high in height, it's walls were full of little ledges and dark openings, but, the floor was all soft clean sand and very comfortable, it appeared to be safe and an ideal place in which to pass the night in peace and safety.

Macormack looked up into the ceiling of the cave, but, it was so high up and dark that he couldn't make out a thing, however it appeared to be empty so he left the interior and went out to tell Nattisa that all seemed to be well.

Little did he know that all was not well, for all the time that he had been looking up into the darkness of the high ceiling, he was being watched by the sleepy eyes of a giant Squid, truly one of the evillest creatures of the sea, besides the Shark! The Squid had been asleep when Macormack first entered the cave, the evil thing was a creature of the night and never ventured out in the daylight, only in the dark did it leave it's abode and go out to hunt for prey.

Macormack had woken it from it's light sleep by making ripples in the water inside the cave, the Squid did not have very good eyesight for it didn't need it when hunting in the dark, it found it's prey by the movement and the ripples that they caused when moving through the water, that was how it had detected the presence of Macormack!! It watched with interest what the Dolphin was doing it couldn't make out a lot, but, it saw enough, it saw the Dolphin go out and Nattisa come in with armfuls of weeds, where she then started laying them evenly on the cave floor, if the evil Squid could have smiled then, it certainly would have done!

The horrid creature went contentedly back to sleep then, it's eyesight may have been poor, but, there was nothing wrong with it's brains, it knew as it slowly closed it's eyes and watched Nattisa laying the weeds on the white sandy floor of the cave, that this was one night when it wouldn't have to go out hunting, the food had come to it, all the Squid had to do was wait for nigh time till it's prey was fast asleep!!

Nattisa busily went about her work unaware of the horror lying asleep above her head in the high reaches of the cave ceiling, she looked at the cave floor and when she was satisfied that the weeds were all evenly spread around and comfortable, she went out into the clearing to wait for Macormack to bring her some food.

She sat in the open just in front of the cave entrance and watched the sea life of the clearing go past her, there were creatures of every kind here, tiny fishes in bright blue colours with a black spot on their sides, large fishes too, swam by her, they were all different colours, but, she liked the vivid yellow ones best with purple zig zag stripes, she also saw sea Horses curling their tails around small weeds, one of the sea Horses was a Male, but, he was carrying a pouch full of young ones ready to be released into the sea, Nattisa watched with interest as this Male creature gently let his pale green offspring free into the current of the sea, whereon they all scattered away in all directions probably never again to meet up in this part of the sea.

Nattisa was still watching all this going on when Macormack returned with the fish for the evening meal, she looked up at his arrival and said, "oh good, here comes the food and I am ready for it too, I am so hungry that I could eat a Shark, fins and all.

Nattisa laid out a large shell plate and on it she put a handful of seaweed, along with that Mussels, Oysters, Shrimps, a nice juicy Crab, a small Lobster and the two Fish that Macormack had brought for her, he on the other hand just ate huge amounts of fish and nothing else, he liked to chase after the fish that he ate, for he loved the thrill of the chase, it was good sport and they tasted all the better for it. After they had satisfied their hunger, they spent the rest of the evening in exploring their surroundings, chatting together and enjoying each other's company. A while later Nattisa said to Macormack, I am getting rather tired now my friend, it has been a long hectic day and I am in need of some rest; besides it is getting dark and all the night hunters will be coming out to dine.

So they entered the cave together and settled themselves down comfortably for the night, once settled they were both soon fast asleep a smile of content on their faces, both had a full stomach and a nice soft bed of fresh weeds on which to spend the night, all around them the sea was calm and soothing, lulling them into a false sense of security, all the daytime creatures such as fish were all dozing too, they were in every nook and cranny, sleeping in the shelter of rocks and weeds, all was peaceful ! Inside the cave the two friends were huddled together, more for company and cosy companionship than warmth, while above their sleeping heads something moved in the darkness of the cave ceiling, the horrid Squid was waking up and coming down from it's roost to dine, it was very hungry and quite prepared to eat them both, but, it made the biggest mistake of it's life in going for Nattisa first!

The vile thing stole down under the cover of darkness, silently it landed on the cave floor and moved stealthily towards it's sleeping victim's, as it approached Nattisa the Squid stretched out it's long tentacles and began to wrap them around her slender body, Nattisa twitched in her sleep as she felt the movement of contact, but, she did not awaken fully because in her sleep weary mind, she thought that it was her friend Macormack snuggling up closer to her for comfort and this thought made her smile, She was half in and half out of sleep when she felt the tentacles tighten around her and begin to squeeze, suddenly, the smile froze on her face as she realised that it couldn't be Macormack cuddling so tightly because he didn't have any arms, she then opened up her sleepy eyes and when she had finally managed to focus them on what it was that was squeezing her, she came face to face with a fiend straight from hell!! It had a huge great wobbly, lumpy head, horrid red evil staring eyes that looked at her hungrily, a pointed beak like mouth which was just opening up to eat her, it's breath was foul and stank of rotted fish, as it squeezed tighter, Nattisa opened up her small mouth and began to give out the wailing scream that was common to all Sprites!

The Squid jumped back and relaxed it's grip on her, it was only for a moment, but, long enough for her to break free from it's grasping limbs, it had jumped back because it had never heard a noise like that wailing scream before in all it's life, and for just one moment the creature had been terrified by that awful high pitched sound!

But, the shock and the fear only lasted a moment, the Squid soon regained it's courage and hunger made the creature loose any fear that it felt for her, however as it moved forward to grab Nattisa in it's tentacles again, the Squid felt a stab of red hot pain in the back of it's head and it realised that the moment of surprise attack had gone, the Dolphin had heard the scream of fear from Nattisa and he was awake immediately and sprang to the defence of the one that he loved!

The Squid tried to turn to face it's attacker, but, it was a creature of wicked stealth not speed and it could not turn quick enough to defend itself, again and again Macormack dived at the horrid thing, and every time his hard nose hit into the soft squelchy flesh he felt it give way with every blow, the terrified Squid tried desperately to get away and to defend itself from the cruel blows, but, it had no chance to escape the onslaught of the angry Dolphin, no chance at all!!

Harder and harder hit Macormack's nose thudding time and again into the flesh of the Squid, suddenly the skin gave way under the force of the attack, Macormack felt his hard nose sinking into the rotten flesh of this evil stinking creature and he felt sick, blood spurted everywhere and still the Dolphin did not cease his attack!

On and on he banged full force into the Squid, he didn't even stop after he knew it was dead in fact, he couldn't stop himself from hitting into it, Macormack had gone a little bit crazy and didn't know what he was doing anymore.

Thoughts kept going through his mind that this creature had dared to even touch let alone try to harm the one person that he loved above all others, he could not accept that and he wanted to kill the vile creature over and over although he knew that it was stone cold dead, by this time nothing much was left of the Squid not even to bury! Nattisa had backed herself into a corner of the cave and pushed right into the recess of the back wall, she watched wide eyed with terror as Macormack repeatedly hit this great lump of bloody mess on the sea floor!

The cave was so thick with clouds of blood and floating green weeds that had been whisked up off the sea floor by the force and turmoil of the attacking Dolphin, she looked at him, but, she did not recognise him as her gentle friend who would not hurt a living thing except a Shark, it frightened her to think that he was capable of such hate and fury, Nattisa had never seen this side of her friend before, not even when he fought off the attacking Sharks before they met Milly, he was never this angry! Suddenly Macormack collapsed in a heap onto what was left of the Squid the anger and the fury were spent and his body completely exhausted at the force of his temper, as Nattisa looked at her friend she saw that he was weeping and great sobs of pain escaped from his weary tortured body, this was another thing she had never seen him do. "Macormack my dear friend, she said, " why do you weep so, I would have thought that you would be happy, you have defeated the creature that you appeared to hate so much, though why I do not know he was only hungry like the rest of us and looked on us as a nice tasty morsel of food...

Macormack raised up his eyes and looked at her, Nattisa drew back from him in fear, for she could see the anger was still there in his eyes, she was afraid that he was going to start to fight with her too, and in her tired and weary state of health that was one thing that she could not cope with at all.

It's no difference at all to me what this vile horrid thing was thinking, or what it wanted, Macormack said angrily, "I care not if it was hungry, I care only that it dared to touch you and tried to harm you," he looked at her sadly, and said, for as long as I live and breathe, none such as this creature shall touch or harm you again, " this I vow to you Nattisa," because I love you," and he started to weep again. "Please don't cry Macormack, Nattisa said, you know that I thank you and that I am really grateful for your saving of my life, I love you too, very much, and as long as I live no matter where you are or what you are doing, I shall always be your friend." Friend," roared Macormack, "my feelings have nothing to do with friendship, don't you understand yet Nattisa, my love for you is not that of a friend for a friend, my love is that of a Male for a Female, I think about you all the time and I need to be near you constantly, for that is how much you mean to me!

If you are out of my sight for too long then I miss you and worry about you all the time, I need to see you and touch you, I am being driven crazy by these feelings that I have for you, and what has made it worse is being afraid to tell you how I felt: It is getting so bad that I no longer think of you as a sea Sprite or I as a Dolphin, to me we are no longer of different races, we are just Male and Female, Boy and Girl and I weep because you do not think of me as I do of you.

"You spend all your time searching the sea for a non-existent mate who you will never find, not of your own kind anyway, while I tag along behind you, not because I want to find your mate for you, but, out of sheer love and devotion and even if you don't return my feelings, I shall stay with you for just as long as you need me!

After he had confessed how he felt to her, Macormack lay on the cave floor absolutely spent, he had exhausted both his body and his feelings for love of her, and was utterly drained of all energy and emotions, he lay unmoving like one that was dead.

Nattisa looked at him and knelt down by his side, "oh Macormack, she said," you don't know what it means to me to hear you speak those words of love, " I gave up trying to find my mate long ago," I have loved you ever since the day that you saved me from being a meal for those hungry Sharks, the day that we met Milly for the first time. Macormack could not believe his ears," I don't understand," he said, if you have loved me so long, then why didn't you tell me, instead of putting me through agony!! Because we are so different in shape and form, said Nattisa, we are from entirely different species and I wasn't sure how you felt about me, I mean what could be more odd a match to mate up with than a sea Sprite and a Dolphin ...

However, on thinking about what the sea Witch said, her exact words were, " an entirely new race will be created, " the likes of which has never been seen before in Middle Earth, I mean what could be more new and unusual than a cross between a Sprite and a bottle nosed Dolphin, Middle Earth will see it's new race yet I'll be bound! Looking at Macormack and smiling, Nattisa said, I think that at long last my search has finally ended, I guess that I have found the mate that I was promised long ago and have since been seeking, we are to be the beginning of this new race of beautiful if not unusual children, for only the great Gods of the sea know what our offspring will look like, all we do know is that they will be loved in as much as their oddly suited parents can love them!

And coming from such a great love like the love that my parents had for each other, then our children can't be anything else, but, beautiful, and smiling at him again Nattisa knew that indeed her search had really and truly ended!!

The plague and the death of her much-loved parents were far away now, finally they were buried in the past where they belonged, now she could only go forward to greet her destiny with open arms and a clear conscious mind, all her feelings of guilt over the death of the people and her parents could be buried in the past with them. For Nattisa had always felt guilty that she had been the only one out of all her people to survive the plague, but, not any more, she was really free from guilt at last! When all had been said that was to say, and no thoughts or feelings left uncovered, Nattisa and Macormack settled down to sleep what was left of the night away, nearby lay the gory remains of the Squid that had met a rough justice from the Dolphin, but, they no longer thought of it any more, their thoughts and dreams were of the future their future together, and what the new race that they would create together would look like, the Squid was buried in the past with all the rest of the horrid things that had happened to them, they only dreamed good dreams of the future !

And snuggled together with the quiet sea gently lulling them off into a deep restful sleep, they spent the rest of the night in complete undisturbed silence....

CHAPTER EIGHT

THE GHOST CITY

After ten long hours of complete undisturbed sleep, the two lovers awoke feeling a whole lot better than they had done the night before, in fact it all seemed like a bad dream the nightmare part being the Squid, the good part being their declaration of love for each other and even that part seemed like a dream!

Macormack looked at Nattisa, and said to her, "was it all a delusion or a dream," for if it was not, then I could swear that I heard you say that you loved me too, after the battle last night when I declared my love for you, was I dreaming when I heard you say that you returned my feelings towards you.

No Macormack, Nattisa said, you were not dreaming, I do return your love and together we shall do and see great things as well as creating a new race, we shall go forth into the future and be remembered for all sorts of deeds and words.

"Now I don't know about you, but, I am rather hungry again so I suggest that we get some breakfast and then resume our journey back to the city of my birth.

Macormack agreed readily with her, for he too was feeling hungry again, he was about to leave the cave to hunt for food when he suddenly noticed something was missing in the cave, looking around him rather puzzled, he said, " where on earth is the Squid," it was there when we went to sleep last night, what was left of it anyway ...

"I don't understand it," he said, the Squid could not have got up and left the cave, there wasn't enough left of it, for it to go anywhere, they both looked over to the spot where they had last seen the remains of the Squid, but, there was nothing left to see, the cave floor had been completely wiped clean, not one piece of flesh or bone remained to prove that the Squid ever existed at all!

Nattisa did not understand it either, "what a mystery," she said, I wonder where it could have disappeared to, I mean we all know that the fishes can eat the dead flesh of any animal, but, surely they can't eat the bones too!!

And that was how it was, not one bit of flesh or bone remained of the huge Squid, even the sand on the sea floor had been smoothed over it was as if the Squid and the battle between it and Macormack had never taken place, looking at each other in wonder neither of them could fathom out where the thing had vanished too, Macormack gave up on the thought, " oh why worry, he said, life is too short to concern ourselves as to what has happened to the vile creature, perhaps it was a dream after all !

So they went about the task of obtaining some breakfast for themselves and wiped the Squid clean out of their minds, they would never know, that as they slept in the early hours of the morning, a great army of silent fishes, both huge and small had entered the cave and devoured every scrap of the Squid, and what they hadn't managed to eat there and then, had been taken away to eat at a later date, bones and all... After they had eaten their meal, Nattisa and Macormack rested for a while for they did not like to swim on a full stomach, it was quite a long rest and they chatted together about different things, then they prepared themselves for the long journey to the South and to Coral City, well-fortified with food and fully rested they began the journey back to the city where Nattisa had been born!

It took them about four weeks of hard swimming to reach the city limits where the cave of the sea Witch was located, which was where they decided to investigate first. Taking all her courage in both hands Nattisa followed closely behind Macormack, he had entered into the cave first to check that there was no danger in there that could harm Nattisa, and even though Nattisa was no coward she was glad to follow behind...

At first the cave seemed dark and gloomy, then their eyes got used to the dull interior, they saw rows of shelves all neatly stacked with bottles of every size and colour, the bottles all had labels on their fronts so that anyone finding them would know straight away what they contained, without having to open up their lids.

The Witch had certainly put her affairs into order, as she had told Nattisa that she was going to do, on the last day that they saw each other, but, of the Witch herself there was no sign that she had ever existed, not one thing, besides her equipment, was left to show that there ever was such a thing as a Witch, residing in this cave.

"I wonder why there are no skeletal remains," said Nattisa, you would think that some little item would be left, if only to prove that she really existed, she was a living thing of flesh and bone , after all this time one would expect there to be no flesh left, but, surely there must be some bone left, unless the plague rotted those away too so that nothing would remain only dust, which would mingle with the sand on the sea floor and it would be as if the Witch and all the other people, including my parents had never been alive at all, "could the Gods be as cruel as that," she thought! After a good long search of the interior of the cave, both of them were convinced that the cave was empty, not even the fishes had visited the home of the sea Witch and Nattisa and Macormack wondered would the rest of the city be like this, a city of ghosts! After one last look around the cave, they left it has they had found it, just waiting patiently for it's next inhabitant, whoever that would be or how long it would take for someone else to come and live in the cave, and learn all the Magic that the sea Witch had to teach in her books and bottles, only heaven would know!!

They left the cave of the sea Witch and cautiously made their way towards the city, but, they needn't have worried for not one living thing did they encounter, no fishes or crabs, not even shrimps or lobsters, nothing dared to disturb the peace and quiet of the dreaded plague city, only the ghosts of the people haunted this lonely place! Nattisa and Macormack searched every building and cave in Coral City leaving the Palace till the last, not one thing of the Sprites remained in those buildings, nothing living or dead to say that this race of people had ever been, the caves and buildings were still and empty, as if they too were waiting for their next occupiers to move in...

On leaving the smaller buildings the two friends made their way at last towards the Palace, they entered the courtyard and looked around, it was all as Nattisa had last seen it, not one thing had altered, the courtyard and all the statues in it were all free from dust or dirt, it was as if even the sand from the sea floor had been afraid to move around within the ghost city, Nattisa could not believe how nothing had changed!

Macormack was just about to enter into the Palace to check it out for danger, when Nattisa stopped him, " wait a moment Macormack," she said, "I know that you wish to go in first to protect me from any danger within, but, I really feel that this is one thing that I have to do for myself for this was my home, where I was born and grew up into the woman that I am now, if I am ever to be the Mother of a new future race then I must enter into here on my own and learn to face up to my past, before I can even begin to think of starting a new future as your mate, for this is where we shall raise the children of this new race and the Palace of my parents shall be our home !

Slowly she entered through the portals of stone that guarded the palace from it's enemies, swimming silently, she made not the least ripple to disturb the peace and quiet that had reigned here for about two years now.

Turning her head from side to side as she swam, looking for danger in every dark room and around every corner, each corridor that Nattisa entered seemed to present her mind with a new danger from an unseen enemy, but, there was never anyone there!

Her heart was banging and thudding in her chest, how Nattisa now wished that she had let Macormack come into the palace with her, but, little did she know he was never far from her, he had been behind her since she first entered the portals of her old home, he was watching her every move from an unseen distance, but, never too far away and always ready and able to pounce on any menace that may confront her!!

Slowly and nervously Nattisa searched all the rooms of the palace, nothing stirred within these forlorn empty walls, not one fish or crustacean, swam in it's waters or crawled on it's floors the place was completely empty and devoid of all life.

When Nattisa had completed her search, she left the palace by the rear entrance and swam back round to the front portals around by the outside of the building, by the time that she arrived back at the entrance where she had started off from, Macormack was waiting patiently for her to return and to all appearances it looked as if he had respected her wishes in remaining where he was and not following her into the palace!

It appears that the palace is empty and has been ever since the destruction of the people by the plague, said Nattisa, to Macormack, it will be an ideal place in which to settle down and start to raise a family, we shall start off living in the palace and then as our race grows and increases, so shall we then branch out into the other buildings and caves of the city, till we eventually create an entire city of descendants! "Wait up a minute, laughed Macormack, aren't you jumping the gun a bit, you are thinking in future terms and we haven't even got settled into the present yet, it will be a long time into the future before our new race will be living in the entire city, and I don't think that we shall be alive to see it, do you?

I think that we should try to get ourselves organized now by moving into our new home, it will take a while to get used to the situation before we can even start to think about having young ones, I know that this used to be your home, but, a lot has happened here and it will probably take you a bit of time to settle down here again. Whereas I have never been here before and it may take me even longer to get used to the place enough to settle down in it, there will be a lot of memories for you here both good and bad, do you think that you are ready yet to stand up to those memories Nattisa, we don't want you having nightmares about the things that you saw happen here! I don't know, replied Nattisa, perhaps I will, or perhaps I won't, only time will tell us that, but, I do know that I was happy more than sad in this place and it is" where I want to stay and live, and also where I want to raise my family.

So they moved into the palace which at first seemed so huge and awesome for just the two of them, but, they soon got used to it and eventually just treated it like the home that it was, coming and going as they pleased and knowing that when they returned that nothing would have invaded their home, no other creature would dare to enter into this place for still the stories were going round the sea creatures that the city was bad news to them, and Nattisa and Macormack liked it that way, complete privacy...

They had been living in the palace for about five months now when Macormack noticed that Nattisa was behaving rather oddly, she was bad tempered and getting very fussy over her food and also her hygiene, she washed herself thoroughly over and over, she insisted that all the shells that were used for plates were spotlessly clean, every morning as soon as she woke up from a restless sleep she would dash to the window of their sleeping room and be sick onto the sea floor, she was also putting on weight ! Macormack watched her and worried about her constantly, but, he would not approach her for he knew that in her state of mind she would only tell him to go away.

Then one day he found her in tears and could stand it no longer, "what is the matter with you Nattisa my love," he asked her, "are you ill or in pain," Nattisa looked at her mate Macormack, and replied, " no my love I am not ill, I am Pregnant!!

Macormack could not believe his ears,"did I hear you right," he said, "or did I just imagine that you told me that you were pregnant! "

"No, said Nattisa, "you are not mistaken, I am definitely with child and have been for a couple of months now, don't ask me how I know this to be true, I just do!" Are you absolutely sure of your condition, I mean how do you know for certain, he asked? Nattisa my love, you have never had a child before, said Macormack, so are you really positive that you have not made a mistake and are coming down with some kind of illness or something, after all you have not been entirely well lately have you!

Nattisa smiled at him, "no, she said, I am not mistaken, I am not coming down with anything, only a bad case of pregnancy that's all, that is why I have been so sick lately it is my condition that is making me off colour, I shall be alright after the first few months have gone over, I know this because I have seen it happen to the other women of my race, when I was a lot younger of course, so I know what to expect. But, what is the matter with you, don't you want me to be pregnant, you sound a bit disappointed and you also sound as though you don't want it to be true, I mean, I thought that this was what we both wanted and why we have come together as mates so that we start a family, the first child of the new race!

"It is," replied Macormack, it is just that I didn't expect it to happen quite so soon as this, we have only been together as mates for about six months and I thought that we would perhaps have just a little more time on our own, before starting a family. I know, said Nattisa, I was thinking along those lines too, but, it appears that it is not up to us to decide when we are to start a family, I rather fear that the fates have taken our future into their charge, it seems that they are not going to give us any more time alone, but, that we are to start the new race a lot sooner than we expected to, the Gods must be in an awful hurry for the new race to take it's place here in Middle Earth, I wonder if they are tired of looking down on an empty city!

When the news had finally sunk in and Macormack had accepted it as true, he was really pleased and terribly exited, how far along do you think that you are, he asked her? " I am not sure, she replied, but, I think that I am roughly about two months along, give or take a few weeks, I can't be certain exactly, although that is how long I have feeling a bit rough and off colour, so I think that's about right, why do you ask!!

"Oh no reason really, I was just wondering if you were too far along to go on a short - journey to see some friends of ours, I am really exited now that I have got used to the idea, I am dying to tell someone else the news, but, who is there to tell besides Toby and Milly, we have no friends in this part of the sea, then thinking about it seriously he added, "in fact if you don't count the Whales, we have no friends at all! Nattisa looked at him, " come on now Macormack don't be so miserable, she said, " this is a time to be happy, you are going to be a Father, that is all that matters, besides the fact that we don't need friends when we have each other, now am I right or not!!

"Yes you are exactly right, declared Macormack, I shall not dwell on it any longer, but, I really would like to tell our friends, so do you think that you would be able to manage the journey to the crater, or would it be too much for you!

"Again I don't know, she told him, the way that I have been feeling lately I fear that such a long dangerous journey could be against the question, are we right to even think of undertaking such a long journey at maybe the cost of our new family, I mean what if something were to happen to our unborn child, I could never forgive myself, could you, and even if we could, I don't think the Gods ever would, we would be in disgrace for all eternity, so I really don't think that I am prepared to chance it.

But, don't worry, if we can't go to visit with them, let us ask them to come and visit with us and when they arrive then we can tell them the news, I mean, there is plenty of room here for them and they could swim faster than us, so they would be here a lot quicker than if we were to go to them, we could send them a message with the fishes who live on the borders of Coral City, "well what do you think of that idea"!

"I think it is a smashing idea, replied Macormack, I shall go at once to the edge of the city limits to ask the fish if they will convey this message to our friends, I do hope that they will, for I can't wait to see them and break the news of our future event. So saying he dashed off to see the fishes and as he swam, he was singing a really happy song, that had been taught to him long ago by his parents before they had both been killed by marauding Sharks, which is why he hated the darn things so much.

At the rate he was swimming, it wasn't long before he was at the city limits and asking the favour of the fishes, who were more than glad to comply with his request, for they too were glad to hear the Dolphin's news and promised him that on their return from the crater, that they would spread the news to the other creatures of the sea, that there was soon to be a new race of people within the city walls again.

The fish also promised Macormack that he and Nattisa would no longer have to live alone, for they would come back to live and swim within the confines of the city, where all the fishes had once lived and swam freely before the event of the plague.

As the fish swam off to deliver the message to Toby and Milly, they advised Macormack to return at once to Nattisa just in case something should happen to her while she was on her own, " you never know, said one of the fishes, anything could befall her in that delicate condition, we shall make all haste to deliver your message to the Whales, they told him, but, what we suggest is that you make all haste to return to your mate and until she safely delivers her baby in about seven months' time, " do not let her out of your sight for one minute, wherever she goes, you go, just to be on the safe side! And with that message of doom to Macormack, the fish swam off to deliver their message to the Whales, Macormack thought about what they had said, then he high tailed it at top speed to get back to Nattisa as fast as he possibly could, and even though he had only been gone for about an hour. he couldn't wait to see her again ...

CHAPTER NINE

THE FIRST BORN

A whole two weeks went by without any sign of their friends arriving, Nattisa and Macormack were starting to be concerned that the fishes had not managed to make the journey to the Whales in safety, or perhaps had not been able to locate the hidden crater, or even if the fishes had just plain forgot all about the message and gone to play with the other creatures of the sea.

But, they needn't have worried on either account, for two days later as they were in the middle of eating their afternoon meal, a great commotion could be heard approaching the palace, and as Nattisa and Macormack went to look through the window they saw in the courtyard below a whole horde of fishes entering the portals of their home, and in the middle of this horde they saw Toby and Milly with not one, but, three babies. The child that Nattisa had helped to be born was swimming in front, while following behind was Toby and Milly swimming side by side with two babies who appeared to be about five weeks old, Milly must have had another set of twins, exclaimed Nattisa to Macormack, "oh how wonderful for them, they must be over the moon about it!

She and Macormack both raced out at the same time to greet their friends, who they had not seen for about eight months now, Toby, Milly, Nattisa said it's so good to see you all again, I see that you have a new addition to the family, as well as your eldest Son, by the way, what did you name your first child and what are the names of these two adorable little darlings, Nattisa asked, Toby?

The first Son we named Triton and the twins names are Corali and Danus, said Toby, Nattisa looked at her friend in awe, you have named your little ones after my parents, she said, what an honour to bestow upon my family, but, why did you so name them, after all you never really knew my parents did you!!

No, replied Toby I never knew your parents, but, I know their Daughter and I am really proud to call their Daughter my friend, after what you and Macormack did for us on the day that we lost our other child, it was the least that we could do to honour both your parents and you, for if they had never brought you into the world in the first place then we would never have known you, and you would never have been there that day to make sure that our stillborn child got the burial that she deserved! We knew what you had done that day for us, for the child told us that you had left and that you had buried his Sister in the grave, although at the time he was too young to understand what it was that you were doing, it was lovely the way that you buried her and arranged her grave with seaweed and boulders over the top, so that it would look completely natural and no one or nothing would know that she was there.

Anyway that is enough about that it is all in the past and that is also enough about us, how are you two going on and what is this important message that you invited us here to hear, the way the fishes were chattering excitedly when they found us it must be just about the greatest news of the century, is it that you have found your mate. " Yes that is partly true, said Nattisa, I have found my mate, in fact I had found my mate for some time, even when we swam the sea together, I had found my mate without even knowing it at the time, but, the main news is that I am pregnant with the first child of the new race, the first and I hope not the last, at least not if I can help it! " I don't understand, said Toby, "what do you mean that you had found your mate for some time without knowing it," are you speaking about Macormack!?

"Yes that is exactly who I am speaking about, and she told Toby the whole story of the Squid, and of the battle where Macormack tore the Squid to pieces, then she told of the declaration of love that Macormack had made to her and also related that she had felt the same way about Macormack, and had done long before he had declared his love for her, in fact ever since the attack of the Sharks.

So that is the whole story from the start to the finish, she said, to her friend Toby, Toby did not know what to say, he was totally dumbstruck, Macormack told me some time ago how he felt about you, Toby finally said, after he had got his voice back, it was when we were in the crater and you were still ill from the Shark attack, he told me that you and he were to be the creaters of the new race and that he had known this for some time, in fact from the first time that he saw you when you saved him from choking to death on the piece of coral that was stuck in his throat, .

He told me all this, but, the only thing was I didn't believe him, you are so different in form that I could never have given it a thought that you and he could have been meant for each other, let alone be the bearers of the new race!!

Please forgive my doubts of you both, but, who could have thought that a sea Sprite and a Dolphin were what the sea Gods had in mind to be mates.

Then he and Nattisa went over to the rest of Toby's family to tell them the good news about the child that was expected, and for Nattisa to be introduced to the youngsters of the Whale family, Macormack had already been introduced as he had made himself scarce while Nattisa had broken the news to Toby.

Milly too could not believe what she was hearing, but, nevertheless she was. very pleased for them and wished them well for the future, good luck, she said, to them, and plenty of it for with young ones to care for you will certainly need lots of luck, then she added looking fondly at her young ones, but, they are well worth it!

I wonder what your youngster will look like, Milly pondered, I would love to see it, for I am filled with curiosity to know what a cross between a Sprite and a Dolphin will turn out like, it will be a very unusual child and that for sure!!

Well then that is settled, said Nattisa, you shall stay with us until the child is born, I am just over three months pregnant by my calculation so the baby will be here in about five or six months' time, we have plenty of room here to accommodate both you and Toby as well as your youngsters, just take your pick of any dwelling that takes your fancy, that is if you can bear to be away from your home for so long. If that is the case then you could stay for a few days visit and return to your home, then when the baby is due I could send the fishes again to let you know, but, you may not arrive here in time for the birth, as it takes about two or three weeks to get here from your home in the crater, anyway you think about it and let me know what you decide to do, for I shall not really mind if you would rather go home to wait. Milly laughed, " no you would not mind if we went home to wait for the news, but, I think that you would prefer that we should stay here with you, wouldn't you, now tell the truth, am I right or am I not, you would rather have me here than miles away! " Yes you are right," said Nattisa, it is not that I don't love Macormack or that I don't want him at the birth, I really do, but, he is a male and when it comes to having babies men are not much good to have around, now are they!!

No they are not, agreed Milly,"why take me for instance, if you had not been there when I was having my first lot of twins, then I am sure that I would have lost more than one calf in childbirth, for there were two males there at the time and not one of them had a clue just what to do, so if you had not realised that the first calf was stuck, then neither I or my eldest Son would not have been here today, we have an awful lot to thank you for Nattisa, and by staying near you till your child is delivered safely into this world then that is the least that we can do !

So you will stay then, asked Nattisa, "yes we will stay, replied Milly, isn't that what I have just been telling you, we shall stay till you have your child and even longer after that, for as long as you need us here in fact, if that's what you want. " Oh yes, said Nattisa, that would be wonderful, not that I don't feel safe with Macormack here, but, I shall feel a whole lot safer to know that I have more than one person on whom I can depend just in case something should go wrong.

Please don't talk like that Nattisa, said Milly, you should think positively that all will go well and that nothing is going to go wrong, and then nothing will go wrong, we shall choose a dwelling not far from the palace so that we shall be in shouting distance just in case you need me for anything, even if it's just for someone to talk to about things that are women's problems, of which males know nothing about! Then laughing again, she and Toby gathered together their brood of youngsters and went to find a suitable cave or building, in which to spend the next few month's till the child of Nattisa and Macormack was born into this world...

The days passed by quite pleasantly in the city and all the friends lived together peacefully with no arguments at all, they played games together and hunted for food together, it was like paradise and life there was so happy and tranquil at least for a while, they were so happy it seemed that nothing could spoil their joy, but, they were wrong, something could and did spoil the happiness of their lives.

It happened one day when the Whale youngsters were playing at chasing each other through the city and around the city limits, Milly had warned them not to go too far away from the city for fear of the dangerous Sharks, but, she did not warn them not to go too far up to the surface of the sea, and in their playing games that is just what they did do, it was a fool hardy thing that nearly cost one of them it's life! The three of them were swimming round and round chasing each other and not noticing that they were getting nearer all the time to the surface of the sea, and were all unaware that a huge bird called a Roc was taking notice of their play, he watched with great interest and much hunger as the young calves got nearer to the surface. He was a huge bird with a wingspan of about eighteen feet and was quite capable of snatching one of the young Whales clean out of the sea, with no apparent hardship to himself, perhaps the eldest Whale might have presented him with a problem, but, the two younger ones were very much easy pickings.

He watched and waited patiently for the moment when one of them was near enough to grab, he had no malice towards these youngsters, he was just hungry and thought of them as food, a nice tasty morsel for a snack and that was all, so he got ready to pounce. Meanwhile down below in the city the Adults had noticed that the young Whales were missing so they started a search, they all split up so that they could cover more ground than if they all stayed together, Nattisa went to look in the buildings to see if the calves were hiding in there, while Milly went to search the vast caves for them. Toby on the other hand went to look around the city limits to see if the calves had strayed out of the safety of the city, all the time he was searching, he was thinking of how he was going to punish them for disobeying orders and worrying their parents! Macormack in his turn went to search the only other place that was left, towards the surface of the sea and that is where he found them, he spotted them just as the huge Roc pounced down to grab one of them for his dinner, as the youngsters looked up and saw the huge shadow of the bird overhead they panicked and instead of all staying together to fight, they all scattered in different directions, that confused the Roc and he didn't know which one to go for first, by the time he had finally made up his mind, "it was too late, Macormack had arrived on the scene and jumping clean out of the water he hit the Roc head on into it's chest completely winding it, that was it for the huge bird, young Whale calves were easy meat, but, it wasn't prepared to take on a full grown angry Dolphin, hungry or not, so it spread out it's huge wings and flew away, watching the bird disappearing into the distance the calves promised never to stray again !!

When the Roc had finally gone, Macormack looked at the young Whales, come, he said, let us get back to the city to let your parents know that you are all okay, but, only just, if I had found you just a couple of minutes later than I did,

I dread to think what might have happened to one of you, then we would be returning to the city with a very different story to tell your parents, a much sadder one than this I fancy. "But, aren't you going to give us a good telling off for straying too far from home, all the calves said in one chorus, "no, said Macormack, I am not your Father, so it is not up to me to tell you off or punish you, all that I can do is relate to your parents the tale such as I know and saw it, the rest is up to them, but, if I was your Father then I would truthfully consider that you have been punished enough, the great Roc frightened you all so much that I would consider that you had all learned your lesson, and that you will not stray away from home again, but, as I said before, I am not your Father and it is not up to me to decide what to do, I will put in a good word for you though with your Father, whether it will do any good though I can't say for sure, but, I will try to persuade him that you have suffered enough !! Thank you for offering to put in a good word for us, said Triton, the eldest of the calves, but, I really feel that it would be better if you just told the story as you saw it, the rest I fear is up to us, we made the mistake of disobeying orders and straying too far from the city, so I think that we should stand up for ourselves and if any punishment is forthcoming, then we should take it like Adults, for we did the wrong thing, we made the mistake and I think that we should own up to it, I for one am ready to take my punishment, any punishment that our Father or Mother dishes out to us, could not be any worse in my book as being a meal for the giant Roc.

"How brave of you to talk like that, said Macormack, you are really growing up into a fine young Whale and you are truly your Father's Son, he will be really proud of you when I tell him of your words, as I who am not your Father am proud of you and I only hope that if my child turns out to be a Boy, I hope that he will be half if not entirely as brave as you are now at this moment.

So the foursome went quietly back to the city, Macormack thinking about when his child was born what would it be like, and the Whale calves thinking about what sort of punishment they would receive from their angry Father, the calves knew that their Mother would not be angry with them, she would be upset and maybe just a little bit ashamed of them for disobeying orders, but, not angry, it was their huge angry Father that they were worried about, after all he was not called a killer Whale for nothing, but, the calves knew that whatever punishment he gave them, he would do it fairly and it would only be because they deserved it !

As they swam down, they could see in the depths below them Coral City, and there waiting for them were their parents and Nattisa, the look on the face of Toby was nearly enough to make the calves turn around and swim off quickly the other way, his eyes were red with anger and his huge body shook with rage, he was absolutely Furious! " Where have you been," his loud angry voice boomed through the sea at his terrified children, and they were not the only ones who were terrified, there was not one fish or creature in that part of the sea who did not take shelter and hide from that voice! " It was awesome in it's fury and as the calves approached their Father, even though they knew that they had done wrong and must accept their punishment, they could not stop their terrified bodies from shaking by the sight of his angry eyes, which were looking at the calves as if he could tear them all to shreds!!

"Again, his voice boomed out, " where have you been and what have you been up to?" And I want the truth mind you, not some tale made up out of your vivid imagination's, now which one of you is going to be adult enough to tell me the truth as to why you disobeyed a direct order, " not to stray from the safety of the city.

The eldest Son looked up at his father and even though he was quivering with fear, right down from his head to the tip of his tail, he spoke up to his father and told him the facts exactly as they had happened with nothing added.

Poor Triton's heart was thumping within his chest and his voice was croaking under the strain of the fear that he felt as he looked up at Toby, but, he still spoke up for both himself and for his Brother and Sister who were too afraid to speak for themselves, besides they were a lot younger than him so being the eldest meant that he had to stick up for them and look after them, which he had nearly failed to do!

"Father, Triton said, I am sorry that we disobeyed your orders, but, we didn't mean to, we were having such fun playing at chasing each other, that we did not realise just how far we were straying from the city, we swam up and up towards the surface and completely forgot about your words of warning until it was nearly too late!

I know that I am the eldest and that I am therefore responsible for my younger brother and Sister, but, I too am still a child and I only wanted to have some fun without having to worry about mine and their safety all the time, I know that I did wrong and even though I am still but, a child, I would like to think that I am man enough to own up to those mistakes and also man enough to be punished when I am in the wrong, which I know that I was today, for it nearly cost the life of one of us and I am before you to do as you will with me, then Triton the child bowed down his head in silence ! As he waited with fear in his heart at what his punishment was to be, he heard the most gentle voice speak, it was his father and Triton had never heard his Father speak in such a voice as this, it was a voice of sorrow and tears, but, also a voice that was filled to bursting with so much pride at his son's words.

Toby said gently to his child, it was Triton the child who bowed down before his Father awaiting his punishment in silence, now let it be Triton the man who raises his head to look me straight in the eyes, " for man you are my Son, and there shall be no form of punishment for you to day or ever again," I think that your brush with death up on the surface of the sea has done enough to punish you don't you "!

Somehow I don't think that you will be leading either your Brother and Sister, or yourself into danger any more, I think that you have learned your lesson and will be much more careful in the future, " oh and by the way, I know that you want some fun too, so did I when I was your age, but, there are ways that you can have fun and be careful at the same time, and smiling at his Son, he said, "if you have got a few hours to spare I will tell you some of them, that's if you would like me to"!

"Oh I would love that, replied Triton, so turning to his other children, Toby said, you two come along too, I don't think that it would do you any harm to learn how to have fun and enjoy yourselves without getting into any danger or trouble, and gathering his children around him with an air of secrecy they all swam off towards the other side of the city to share some private ways of having fun, handed down from Father to Son and to Daughter, right through from Toby's ancestors to the present generation.

When the four of them had gone off into the deserted part of the city, the children to learn some of the games that their Father had played when he was little, and Toby to forget that he was grown up with children of his own, but, to pretend that he was a child himself again doing all the things that he used to do with his father, now it was the other way around he was the father, how time flies by, he thought, it doesn't seem like two minutes ago that my Father taught these games to me and now here I am Twenty years later teaching them to my children, life is a funny old thing, he said !!

As Nattisa, Milly and Macormack watched the four of them vanish into the distance, the three friends looked at each other and laughed, Toby is such a dear isn't he, said Milly, to Nattisa, his bark is far worse than his bite, he never really meant the children any harm, he was just worried for their safety, and even if Triton hadn't spoke up to him like that Toby would not really have punished them for what they did.

" I know that, said Nattisa, you forget Milly that I have known Toby for a long time, he was born around here and he and I grew up together, we played games of hide and seek together around these parts and I know that he could never hurt a thing, he is too gentle and kind, and despite his size

115

which would put the fear into anyone, I have known him too long to even think that he would dream of hurting a child especially his own!

And now if you will excuse me, said Nattisa, I think that I will go and have a lie down for I am feeling a bit tired and rather ill, and with that statement she fainted clean away, Milly and Macormack didn't know what to do for the best, but, they knew that the one thing that they shouldn't do was panic, they tried to lift her calmly and carry her gently to the palace to put her to bed.

All was going well as they gently carried her back towards the city, they were through the portals at the entrance to the city and were nearly at the palace when Milly first noticed the cloud of blood trailing behind them, " Macormack stop a minute, I think that Nattisa is bleeding, let us examine her before we go any further.

"What do you mean, Macormack exclaimed, " why is she bleeding, what can have happened, " do you think that we could have scratched her on the rocks as we were passing by," " I don't remember bumping her at any time, do you?

"No we did not bump her, said Milly, nor did we scratch her, we have been really careful as we have carried her, she examined Nattisa very gently, and said, there are no cuts or marks on any part of her body that would account for the blood, I don't know for sure just what is wrong, but, it appears as if the blood is coming from inside Nattisa's body, and though I don't know much about these things, in my opinion I would say it was one of two things, either the baby is ready to be born or that Nattisa is going to miscarry and either the child is going to be born too soon, or that she is going to lose it and it will be stillborn, as was mine when I had the twins! " Have you any idea how far on Nattisa is into her pregnancy, if we had a rough idea when she was due to have the child it would help a lot and take out all the guesswork!

Macormack tried to remember how long it had been since Nattisa first told him that she was going to have a baby, but, so much had happened since then that he just couldn't think, also he was very afraid for Nattisa and that fear muddled his thoughts.

"Oh I don't know, he said tearfully, I just can't think straight and I am so afraid that something is going to happen to either Nattisa or the baby, I don't want anything to happen to either of them, "I love her so much and I do so want to be a Father and I just can't remember when Nattisa first told me the news," oh what are we to do"! Well, replied Milly, one thing that we must not do is panic, we must be calm and get her to the palace and into bed as fast as we can, then all we can do after that is pray that both Nattisa and the child will both be okay, she is young and strong and I think that she will cope well under stress of pain, but, about the baby we shall just have to wait and see, if the Gods are eager to get the new race well and truly implanted into Middle Earth, then I feel that both Mother and child will survive !!

So they lifted her gently again and made their way as best they could to the palace bedroom that both she and Macormack shared together, once into the room they both laid her down on a bed of nice soft fresh seaweed and made sure that she was comfortable, once that was done Milly ushered Macormack out of the room, he wanted to stay with Nattisa, but, Milly would not hear of it, you have done your share of the work in helping to get her here, she said, now leave the rest up to me and Nattisa, for this is Woman's work and there is no place here for a Male, now please go somewhere and let us get on with it, for I have a feeling that tonight is going to be the longest night of all our lives, especially Nattisa's and yours !

Once she had finally got Macormack to leave the room, even though he went out sulking he had to go, for Milly left him with no choice in the matter at all, but, once he was gone then Milly got down to the job in hand, to deliver Nattisa safely of her baby! The first thing that she had to do was to bring Nattisa around from her faint, for she would need Nattisa conscious and with all her facilities in order, Milly herself could only help in part, all the real hard work would be up to Nattisa and she would need to be fully awake and conscious for that, if the baby was to be born alive!

Milly bent over Nattisa and began to shake her gently and call her name softly, so as to avoid too much shock to Nattisa when she came round from her faint, when this gentle approach did not work Milly shook her a bit harder this time, and called her name a little louder, still Nattisa lay in a deep faint with not one flicker of her eyelids to show that she was still, in the land of the living.

This is no good, thought Milly none of this is working, I must try another way to bring her around, for bring her around I must, or else the child she is carrying will die! So on deciding that the gentle approach was not working, Milly knew that she must try to wake Nattisa with special herbs growing near to the outskirts of the city, she checked to see if Nattisa was still alright before popping out to have a quiet word with Macormack, for it would have to be he that brought the herbs that Milly needed to awaken Nattisa, Milly knew that she could not go for them, as it would mean leaving Nattisa alone or worse still she thought, leaving her with a panic stricken Dolphin ! She came out of the room and closed the seaweed curtain over the entrance so that Macormack could not see what was happening inside, then she told Macormack what it was that she wanted and described the herb in great detail, so that he would not return with the wrong thing, when she had finished her description Macormack looked at her in a rather mystified way, " why did you describe the herb to me in that way," he said, " do you not trust me to know what herb you are talking about, or do you think me stupid, I am not a little child to be spoken to in such a stupid way"!!

"I am sorry," said Milly, I did not realise that I was doing anything, other than making it known to you exactly which herb that I wanted you to bring for me, I meant no harm, nor did I wish to insult you, as you obviously think that I have!

I did not know that you knew the herb to which I was referring, if I had known that then I wouldn't have described it to you in such detail, but, even so what are you doing still here with me, arguing about it, I say again that I am sorry if I offended you, I know that you are in a touchy mood at the moment and I no doubt are feeling very vulnerable, but, I have no time for any of this at the moment, if your mate and child are to survive this night then I need this herb as like at this exact moment right now, it is of the utmost extreme urgency that you bring me this healing herb immediately!

Milly had hardly finished speaking, when Macormack realising the urgency of her words took off with all haste to bring back the herb that Milly needed to bring Nattisa out of her faint, and once that was done Milly could then get on with the long tiring job of helping Nattisa to deliver her baby safely, without harm to either of them. Macormack swam at top speed to the spot where the herbs grew and within minutes was back beside Milly handing them to her, " do you think that these will do the trick, he asked her, or have I not brought enough for the purpose in hand!

"Yes I think that these will bring Nattisa around quite nicely, don't worry you have brought more than enough to make her recover quickly and safely, and with those words Milly disappeared behind the seaweed curtain to get on with the job of saving Nattisa and her unborn child, for the sake of the new race, she knew that she mustn't fail!! After Milly had gone back into the room with Nattisa, Macormack did not know what to do with himself, he knew that he had to keep busy so that he wouldn't keep thinking about what was going on in that room, he went off for a swim, but, he kept wondering if Nattisa was awake yet, if the herbs had done the trick in bringing her round, was she or the baby in any pain, or did Milly need any help that required his presence, all sorts of thoughts were whirling around in his mind and it gave him an headache !

Slowly he entered the palace again and approached the bedroom where Nattisa laboured in pain to give birth to his child, that was his hope anyway, he did not even want to think about the possibility of what Milly had said, about the child being stillborn, the Gods would never allow for such a thing to happen to one of the new race surely! If only I could see what was going on in there, he thought to himself, but, perhaps Milly is right, I know that I could be not much help and might even get in the way, I mean what do I know about delivering babies, but, I just wish that I could be with my loved one in her hour of need, perhaps I shall go off to find Toby and the children and tell them what is happening at the palace, I may feel better to have someone with me to talk to while I wait for news, and with that he went off to find Toby...

He found his friend in one of the larger caves playing games with his children, they all stopped playing when they saw the Dolphin approaching them with such a worried and frightened look upon his face, they knew that something was wrong so they came to him. " What is the matter, asked Toby, " you look as if you have the troubles of the whole sea upon your shoulders, are we under attack from some great creature or what!!

"No we are not under attack, replied Macormack, it is much worse than that, and he told them everything that had transpired since they had gone off together to play.

"Oh how awful for you, said Toby, don't be too concerned though, Milly has a good idea what she is doing and will not let anything happen to either Nattisa or the baby, not if she can help it, if the child can be helped into this world safely, then Milly is the one to do it, stop worrying and you will see, you shall soon be looking at your new offspring and then you will wonder what all this fuss was ever about!!

After Macormack had given the herbs to Milly, she had gone back into the bedroom to find that Nattisa was still out cold, so she got herself busy in preparing the herbs to see if they would bring the Sprite back into this world fully conscious.

Milly crushed the herbs with one of her flippers into a shell container and placed it directly under the nose of Nattisa, within a few moments of the aroma penetrating her nostrils Nattisa began to be aroused from her faint and began coughing, as the herbs that she was smelling were very strong with a nasty pungent smell that took her breath. "What is happening, moaned Nattisa, " where am I and what is that awful smell? " Don't worry Nattisa, said Milly, it is only herbs that you smell and you are in your own bedroom here in the palace, you fainted and I couldn't make you wake up, so I had to crush some pungent herbs to bring you around from your faint!

"Now I must ask you, how far on do you think that you are in your pregnancy, I have got to know because I think that you have started in labour and if you have gone full term then the baby will be alright, but, if you are not full term then you may lose it! " Why I think that I am roughly about eight and a half months along, replied Nattisa, but, I am not sure for certain, it could be more or it could be less, are you really positive that I am in labour or could it be a false alarm..

"No I am not absolutely positive, said Milly, but, I have a good idea that you may be in what we call the first stages of labour, because your waters have broken! If I am right, because this is your first baby, it may be a long time before the birth or then again in some cases, it could be no more than a few hours or minutes, no one knows for certain just how long it takes for labour to be completed when it's your first, or for that matter even when it's your second, but, I have no doubt at all that the child it's self will let us know when it is coming, all we can do is wait!!

And wait they did, two hours later with no sign whatever of the baby coming, the two of them were just beginning to think that it had been a false alarm when suddenly Nattisa had her first pain, she jumped up in bed clutching her stomach and cried out in agony the pain was unbearable, this was just the first of many such pains, each one a little harder and more unbearable than the last, it took exactly four hours of labour then came the greatest pain of all and the child was born into the world of the sea, Milly looked in awe at the tiny creature lying at the foot of her Mother's bed and she could not believe what she was seeing," why I must be dreaming, she said, will someone please wake me up, " for I swear that I am dreaming, it can't be true !!

"What is the matter," exclaimed Nattisa,"is there something wrong with my child," "is it a freak or what, please tell me what is wrong, I must know, "what does it look like," "I knew that nothing good would come of a mating between a Sprite and a Dolphin! "Oh you are wrong there Nattisa, said Milly, something good has come from your mating, the two of you have created a being such as I have never seen before and it is so beautiful that I could never in a million years describe it to you, you shall have to see it for yourself to believe it!!

Nattisa began to ease herself up onto her elbows so that she could see just what it was that Milly was talking about, when she felt another pain, though not quite as bad as the first lot of pains, it was still bad enough to make her cry out, " oh what is : happening now, she cried, don't worry, said Milly, it is probably the afterbirth coming out, but, she was wrong, for within a few minutes Nattisa had given birth to another baby, and after that another, then another, Four babies, Milly exclaimed, " you have had four babies, is that the last or are you going to produce some more"!!

"Four, she kept repeating in disbelief, and each one just as beautiful as the rest, but, it beats me what sex they are, for they all look exactly alike, you cannot tell if they are Male or Female, but, they are the most beautiful creatures that I have ever seen! When Nattisa was sure that she was not going to give birth to any more babies, she at long last propped herself up onto her elbows to look at her offspring and this is what she saw, lying there at the foot of her bed were four tiny babies, each one of them had the top half in the form of herself as a sea Sprite, whereas the bottom half of them from the waist downwards was all fish, they had beautiful Orange coloured fish tails and each one of them had their mother's blonde hair and blue eyes.

All four of them were identical in looks and Nattisa decided that Milly was right, you could not tell what sex they were, not yet anyway, perhaps when they got a bit older than they would probably take on the looks of either Female or Male, but, till then Nattisa could not give a name to any of them, so she decided to call them for the time being, her Merbabies, till each one developed the characteristics of either Male or Female, then they could be known by the name of Mermen and Mermaids, the new race !! Of course she would give them all individual names of their own, depending on what sex they turned out to be, but, the new race themselves would be names Merpeople!

She looked down at her beautiful babies and her heart sang with happiness and was so full of pride at what she and Macormack had produced together, Nattisa thought back to the words that she had spoken earlier on, when she had thought that Milly had meant that she had given birth to a freak, she was sorry now for those words, which had been spoken in ignorance and haste, and she begged the Gods to forgive her for not having any faith in their plans for the continuation of Middle Earth, she might have known that the great ones would not have let her give birth to anything that looked like a freak .. Thank you very much Milly for all that you have done for me here today, said Nattisa, it will be a long time before I forget this day, for every time I look at my children I shall remember this day and I shall never stop being your friend, It is only a favour returned, said Milly, for every time that I look at Triton, I remember what you did for me when I was giving birth to my twins, and I too shall always be your friend, "now I think that it is time that we put Macormack out of his misery and told him that he is a Father to Four bouncing babies, I think that he too will need a sniff of the pungent herbs to help him to recover from the shock, and bring him around when he faints " !!

"Oh no," exclaimed Nattisa, " please don't leave me on my own with them and she looked fearfully at her new brood of babies, " I am afraid of them, she said! If there had only been one of them, then that would have been alright, I could handle one baby, but, not four of them, that is a little more than I can manage. " Don't worry, laughed Milly, I would not dream of leaving you on your own with your babies, not so soon after you have just given birth to them, nor will you be left on your own later on to raise them, " I know that you will have Macormack to help you to raise the little ones, but, somehow I don't think that the two of you will be enough, " do you"!

So if you would like me to, I shall stay around and help you in every way that I can till you are able to manage on your own, for they won't stay so tiny and helpless for long you know, in a very short while they will have grown enough to be able to look after themselves, but, till then I will always be close by to help all I can! "Oh thank you so much Milly, that is really good news, said Nattisa, I know that I shall have Macormack as you say, but, they are not much help when it comes to rearing babies and I would much prefer to have you around to help me.

"What about Toby and your young Sons though, will they not object to your staying here for so long, said Nattisa rather worriedly, do you not think that they would much prefer to be back at home in the crater than here looking after us? " NO I do not think that they would prefer to be back in the crater, said Milly, we all had a long talk on the matter just yesterday evening, as a family should discuss things that are of importance to their happiness and wellbeing, well to cut a long story short, we all agreed that we have been happy here and we are safe from all enemies as long as we don't stray too far from the city limits, there is plenty to do here so we are not bored in any way, so we have decided as a family that we shall stay here with you for as long as you want us to, besides the crater will still be there whenever we are ready to go back there and it will always be our true home, so stop worrying and take advantage of us while you can!

"That would be wonderful for you all to stay here, exclaimed Nattisa, and don't worry I fully intend to take advantage of your very generous offer, even if I had only had the one child I would still have needed your help, but, now I need you more than ever, besides your Sons will help my little ones in their play and that way they will come on quicker and grow up faster and before you know it, you will soon be back in your own home, not too soon though I hope!!

"Now tell me, Nattisa asked Milly, if you are not going to leave me alone with my new brood, just how are you going to get a message to the others about the babies?!

"Ah, said Milly, in a very mysterious voice, I planned all that while you were out cold still unconscious, I had no intention of leaving you anyway after your baby was born, "or babies as it has turned out in this instance," so while you were out for the count I asked some fishes would they mind hanging around till after the birth and take a message to the others, they have been waiting to take that message ever since you went into labour and they are still waiting right now at this very minute. In fact I thought that they might not have needed to take it, I rather thought that Macormack may have come back for himself to check if there was any news, but, he may not have thought that it would have been so quickly over, he may think that you are still in labour and he hated to see you suffering so much, that is why he went out of the way, but, I thought that he would have returned by now, "still it won't take a minute for the fishes to find them and to give them the message.

So after taking a peek at the babies to see if they were alright, "which they were," all four of them were fast asleep with dreamy smiles upon their tiny lips, that was how they would spend the first few months of their early lives, asleep and dreaming!

Once Milly had convinced herself that the little ones were fine, she popped across to the open window hole of the bedroom and told the fishes of the news, then asking the excited fishes if they could impart that news back to Macormack and the others, she went back to be with Nattisa and the four little Merbabies whose unusual looks and great striking beauty truly amazed and fascinated her, as Milly looked down upon these lovely creatures who were to be the future race of this world and the future population of this city, she wondered to herself, that if they were so utterly beautiful and fascinating at this tender age, " then what on earth would they be like when they were fully grown adults, "Middle Earth is in for a real treat, she thought, but, Milly also wondered if they would be vain and selfish as their ancestors the Sea Sprites had been, somehow she couldn't imagine that being the case at all ! Milly was just about to say something to Nattisa about her thoughts, but, as she looked across to speak to her, the words fell silent on her lips unspoken as she saw that the poor exhausted Sprite was fast asleep and dead to this world...

"Suddenly Milly heard a huge commotion of happy chattering and laughter heading towards the bedroom from up the corridor, she knew then that the others had received the message taken by the fishes and the poor Whale thought, " oh no, they are all going to come in making a huge noise and wake up both the babies and Nattisa who were all thoroughly tired out from their long and painful ordeal, and Milly knew that she must act quickly and go out into the corridor to meet up with Macormack, also Toby and her three Sons to stop them all from stomping noisily into the room and waking up the five sleeping beauties!!

So after she had checked to make sure that none of the sleeping five had been woken up yet by the loud noises outside of the room, Milly rushed to the doorway and out into the corridor with great haste, so much haste in fact that she bumped right into Toby, he had been at the front of the noisy troop of happy reveller's and got the full force! " What on earth is the matter with you Milly," he exclaimed, " why are you in such a mad rush, then he looked at her worriedly, "is there something wrong, he asked? No not yet, replied Milly, but, there soon will be if you lot do not quiet down and have a little thoughtfulness for the poor Sprite in there, not to mention the babies, they have all gone through so much over the last few hours and they are exhausted, every one of them is at this moment fast asleep so if it's not too much trouble would you mind keeping your noisy celebrations till later on, after they wake up!!

Macormack was looking at Milly with a puzzled expression on his face, " I don't think that I must have heard you right, he said to Milly, " I could have sworn that you said babies and not baby, but, I must have misunderstood your words, what with all the noise that was going on perhaps my ears were trying to deceive me!

"NO, said Milly, it was not your ears that were mistaken, you heard me quite rightly, I did definitely say babies, Nattisa has given birth to more than one child, but, I thought that the fishes would have told you that, for that was the message that I asked them to give to you, if they differed my message to you in any way then I shall give them all such a tongue lashing as they have never had before in their entire lives!

Macormack said, " no please don't do that Milly, it may have been that in all the excitement I didn't hear what they were saying to me properly, it was good of them to come looking for us in the first place to give us the message, so please don't scold them for doing a good deed, " now tell me, has Nattisa given birth to Twins or what!!

"No, answered Milly, Macormack I think that you should take stock of your mind for a while, for you are in for a great shock, Nattisa has not given birth to two babies or even three, your mate Nattisa has produced a total in all of Four babies!!"

The poor Dolphin was dumbstruck, he looked at the Whale and his mouth was wide open, for once in his life he could not think of one thing to say, then slowly as the shock subsided and he got his wits together, he said in a croaky voice, Four babies, did you say Four babies, I can't believe it, but, how are we going to manage, he said in horror!

"Don't you worry your head about that Macormack, said Milly, that is all arranged we have decided that Toby and myself, and also our Sons shall stay here for as long as you need us to help out with the rearing of your little ones, " now if I was you, I would go as quietly as you can into the room where your loved ones are sleeping to have a look at your beautiful new Family, for beautiful they truly are, you and your mate have done well for the new race of Middle Earth, now go and see them for yourself !

Slowly the Dolphin parted the seaweed curtain that hid the bedroom from the corridor he glided through the curtain like a ghost, so quietly and silent that none of the sleeping persons within were aware of his presence as he watched them in their sleep. Macormack looked down upon the faces and forms of the tiny new born infants and their beauty took his breath, they were utterly exquisite and he too had never seen any others like them in this or any other part of the sea, he was so proud that he a lowly Dolphin had taken part in the creation of these beautiful creatures.

He examined them in minute detail as they slept and noted the pure clear skin so pretty and smooth, he noted too that they had the blonde hair of their Mother, but, their tails were orange in colour and Macormack thought to himself, they have many characteristics of their mother, but, I can't see where I have contributed to their creation, they are not like me in any way shape or form except for having tails, which are not even the same shape or colour as mine, I don't understand it at all!!

Then he looked down upon Nattisa and thought, " oh Nattisa, they are my babies as well as yours aren't they, "I wish that she would wake up then I could ask her, "why none of our children look like me, I do hope that they are mine, he thought, but, who else's could they be, Nattisa could not have gone with anyone else, bedsides there being no one else for her to go with, I truly trust in her to be faithful to me, so why do the infants not resemble me in any way it is a mystery ...

Macormack left the room feeling in one sense very happy and excited, and in another sense worried and puzzled, in fact he had very mixed feelings indeed...

Well," said Milly, what do you think of your new babies, are they not beautiful?! " Yes," answered Macormack, they are indeed very beautiful just like their Mother in fact, Milly stared at him, then why are you so miserable and looking so puzzled, she asked, is there something wrong with the little mites, that you have noticed and I have not, ". please tell me why you look so worried and upset:

"It is nothing, said Macormack, "well almost nothing," I was just wondering why none of the babies look like me, "I mean none of them have the colour of my tail or anything and I just can't understand it," they have Nattisa's skin colouring and her blonde hair, also I bet they have the same colour of eyes as her, even though I can't see this as they are still asleep, but, I bet they do!!

I just can't understand why they have nothing that resembles me, I mean, I did make a contribution to their creation didn't I, at least I hope that I did!

"Oh Macormack, exclaimed Milly, "what on earth are you saying," " do you realise what you are accusing Nattisa of doing," " why you of all things should realise just what you mean to Nattisa, you know that she loves you and thinks the world of you," and if the fact that none of your children look like you is all that's worrying you, then take a look at my Sons, I know that Toby is their Father, but, not one of them looks like him in the least, they don't look like me either, but, you don't see us worrying do you, not all children have to look like their parents thank God!!

They were still discussing the lack of similarity between Macormack and his children, when suddenly a weary voice sounded from within the bedroom, " Macormack is that you and Milly that I can hear talking loudly, " what on earth are you both going on about in such a loud tone of voices," " don't you know that we are trying to get some rest !1 " Yes it is myself and Milly that you can hear talking my dearest one, said Macormack, and we are sorry if we disturbed you from your sleep, but, we did not realise that we were talking quite so loudly, we shall try to be a bit quieter so that you can continue your sleep undisturbed, we have not woken the little ones too I hope, he said softly. " No you have not woken them up, Nattisa said, they are all still fast asleep and really exhausted from their long struggle to come into this noisy world, except that it wasn't quite so noisy till you and Milly started to argue amongst yourselves!

We were not arguing Nattisa, said Milly, whatever gave you the idea that we were, we just had a difference of opinion that's all, there was no way that it was an argument... Well it makes no difference if it was an argument or not, said Nattisa, " it is too late now anyway, I am awake now and the babies are just opening their eyes too, so you may as well all come in to have a look at the first born of the New Race!!

On hearing these words Milly parted back the seaweed curtain to allow the others to enter into the bed chamber to see the new born Merbabies in all their glory... " Oh aren't they lovely exclaimed Toby, as he squeezed his great bulk into the not so large chamber and rested his eyes upon the babies, " I have never seen their like in all the kingdom of the seas or oceans that I have swum in, they are unique!

"That is supposed to be the whole idea my dear, said Milly, that is why they are called the New Race, because there is no other beings entirely like them in the entire world, these children are to be the start of an entirely fresh and new population in this part of the sea, they have got to be beautiful and unique to compare with the race that used to flourish in this city, for even though the Sprites were childish and selfish as a race, they too were unique in their own way and also very beautiful as we can see ! As Milly said this, she was looking at Nattisa, who even though was grateful for the compliment paid to her was blushing like a bright red coral bush...

"Thank you kindly Milly for those words, said Nattisa, "I know that at this moment in time that I am not looking at my best, but, those words said with such sincerity have made such a real great difference to the way that I am feeling and I thank you very much for them, " I also thank Toby for the compliment to my babies, I too think that they are beautiful and unique, but, I have one question to ask you all and it is a hard question that is really troubling me greatly, in fact it is making me ill with worry! Milly looked at Nattisa with curiosity, " well ask away my dear friend, she said to Nattisa, ask away, and if it is within our power to answer that question then we shall do so gladly, for we are here to help you in any way that we can!!

"I will ask it, said Nattisa, but, you must give me a little time to get my words in the correct order, for it is a very embarrassing question that I have to ask and I am not quite sure how to word it, just give me a moment to compose my thoughts ....

After Nattisa had been silent for a minute or two, she was finally composed enough to ask her question, she looked at them all, but, in particular at Milly, how on earth am I going to feed them all enough to make them grow into good strong adults, she asked? ". I mean without being rude, I have only two breasts and yet I have four babies, now you tell me how I am going to make that work out, because two into four won't go!

Milly nearly exploded with laughter, "oh Nattisa, you do say the funniest things at times, if that is all that is worrying you then you can rest at ease, for that is one problem that is easily solved, I worked all that out when you were sleeping..."

"I knew that you would have a problem in that department, so to solve it for you, I have decided to feed two of them myself with the milk that I have left from my own birthing, if that is alright with you, that is!!

"That would be fine with me, said Nattisa, " I don't think that I would have any problems with that at all, as Nattisa finished speaking the babies began to cry with hunger, Milly smiled at Nattisa, well I think that we should get all this lot out of the bed chamber, she said, indicating at Macormack and Toby, also at her children, " I think that by the way in which your babes are crying, that we had better put that idea into practice don't you, now come along now, she said busily to the others," " off you all go now, while we women get on with the job of feeding the little ones!

As Macormack was ushered out of the room with the rest of them, he looked back and saw Nattisa gathering one of the babies into her arms to feed it, while Milly got on with the job of feeding one of the other babies, " what a wonderful sight, he thought, he now no longer cared that his offspring did not resemble him in any way, Macormack only cared that he loved them all, especially their mother, as he looked lovingly upon the scene within the bedroom nursery, he thought to himself, " my job is over now, theirs is just beginning, " of course I shall help to rear the little ones as much as I can, but, that is one job that I cannot help out with, even if I wanted to, he added!!

"I don't think that we shall have any more children, thought Macormack to himself, considering the bad time that Nattisa had I think that four is more than enough.... But, he and Nattisa did have more children, and those children went on to have babies of their own, so it went on down through the ages, right up to the present time, when tales of Mermaid and Mermen sightings are still reported!

Nattisa lived to a ripe old age with Macormack, the once sad Sea Sprite was now truly happy that her race of people would be remembered always as the doomed race that created a new race, a great race of half Sprite and half Dolphin, the race of the Mermaids.... Now at long last Nattisa knew that what the Witch had told her was true, she knew now why she had been spared from death by the plague, and in this knowledge she was entirely and utterly happy!!

THE END

Made in the USA
Monee, IL
26 April 2021

66956024R00083